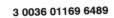

SuperGirl

cosmic adventures in the 8th grade

STONE ARCH BOOKS
a capstone imprint

STONE ARCH BOOKS™

Published in 2013
A Capstone Imprint
1710 Roe Crest Drive
North Mankato, MN 56003
www.capstonepub.com

Originally published by DC Comics in the U.S.
in single magazine form as Supergirl: Cosmic
Adventures in the 8th Grade #4.
Copyright © 2013 DC Comics. All Rights Reserved.

Cataloging-in-Publication Data is available at the
Library of Congress website:
ISBN: 978-1-4342-4720-9 (library binding)

Summary: A little orange cat with a big attitude
shows up on the scene, but is he friend or foe?
And Lena makes a discovery that may change her
friendship with Linda forever.

STONE ARCH BOOKS

Ashley C. Andersen Zantop *Publisher*
Michael Dahl *Editorial Director*
Donald Lemke *Editor*
Heather Kindseth *Creative Director*
Brann Garvey *Designer*
Kathy McColley *Production Specialist*

DC COMICS

Jann Jones & Elisabeth V. Gehrlein *Original U.S. Editors*
Adam Schlagman *U.S. Associate Editor*
Simona Martore *U.S. Assistant Editor*

DC Comics
1700 Broadway, New York, NY 10019
A Warner Bros. Entertainment Company

Printed in China by Nordica.
1012/CA21201277
092012   006935NORDS13

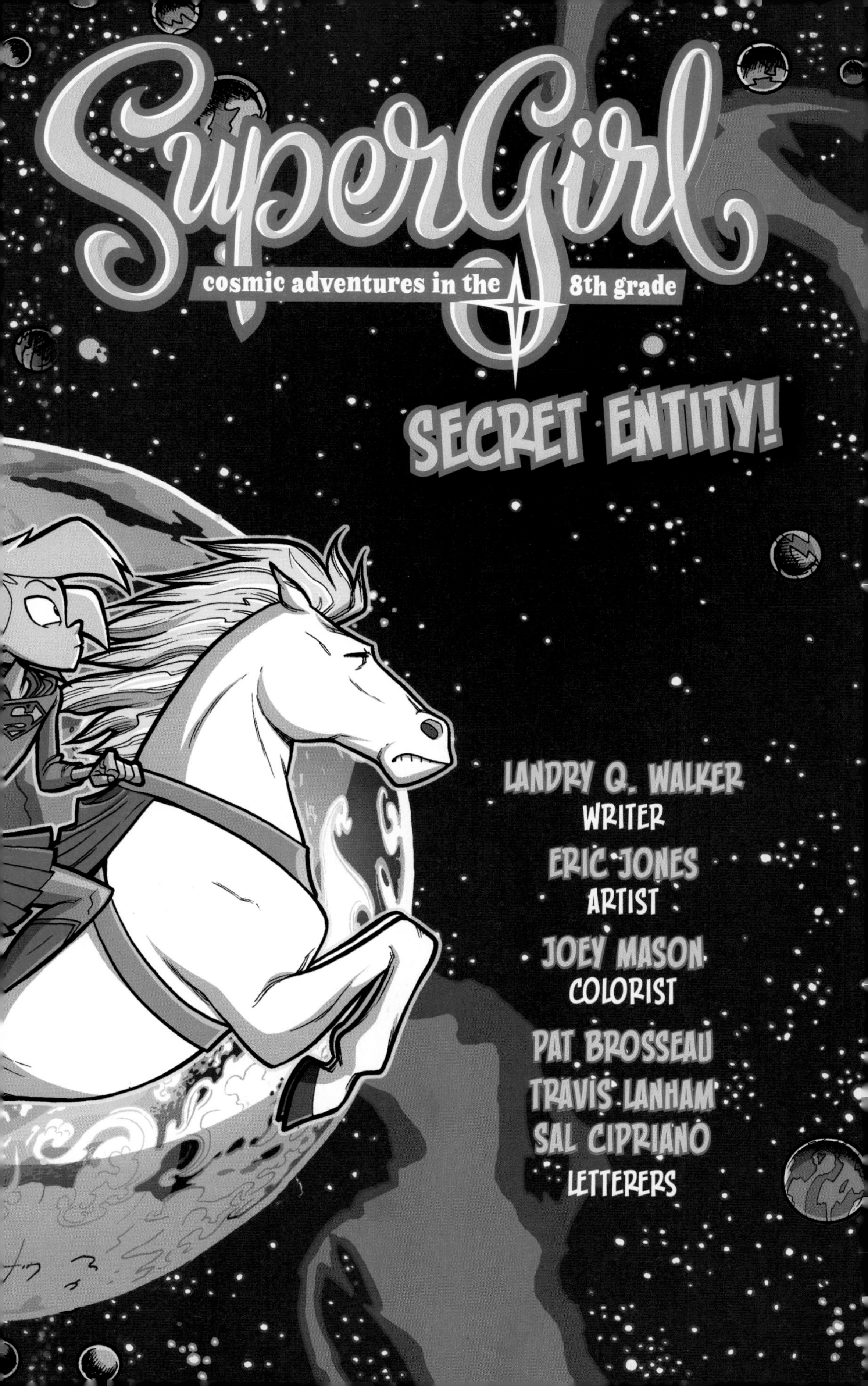
SuperGirl
cosmic adventures in the 8th grade
SECRET ENTITY!
LANDRY Q. WALKER
WRITER
ERIC JONES
ARTIST
JOEY MASON
COLORIST
PAT BROSSEAU
TRAVIS LANHAM
SAL CIPRIANO
LETTERERS

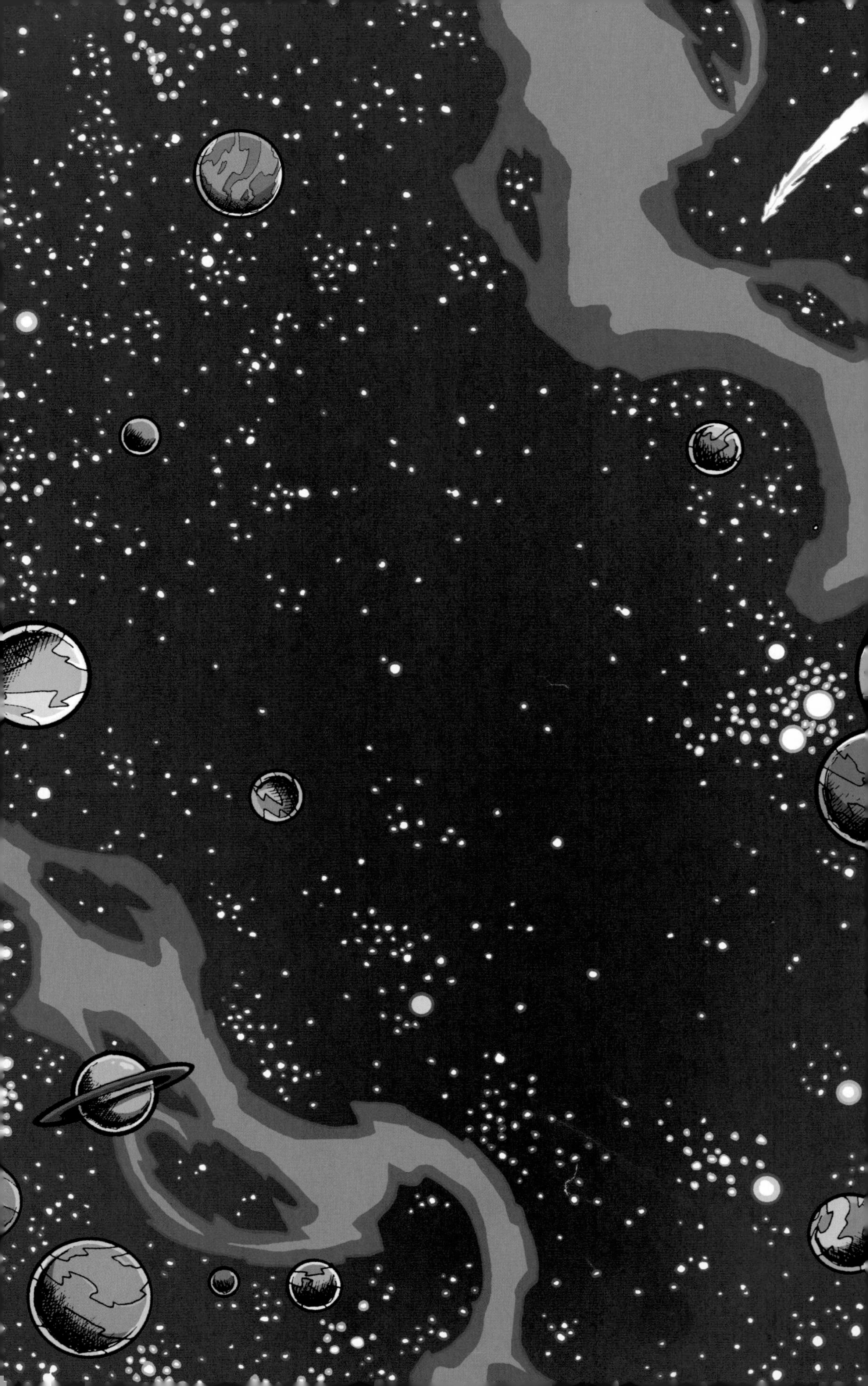

PART 1: "SECRET ENTITY!"

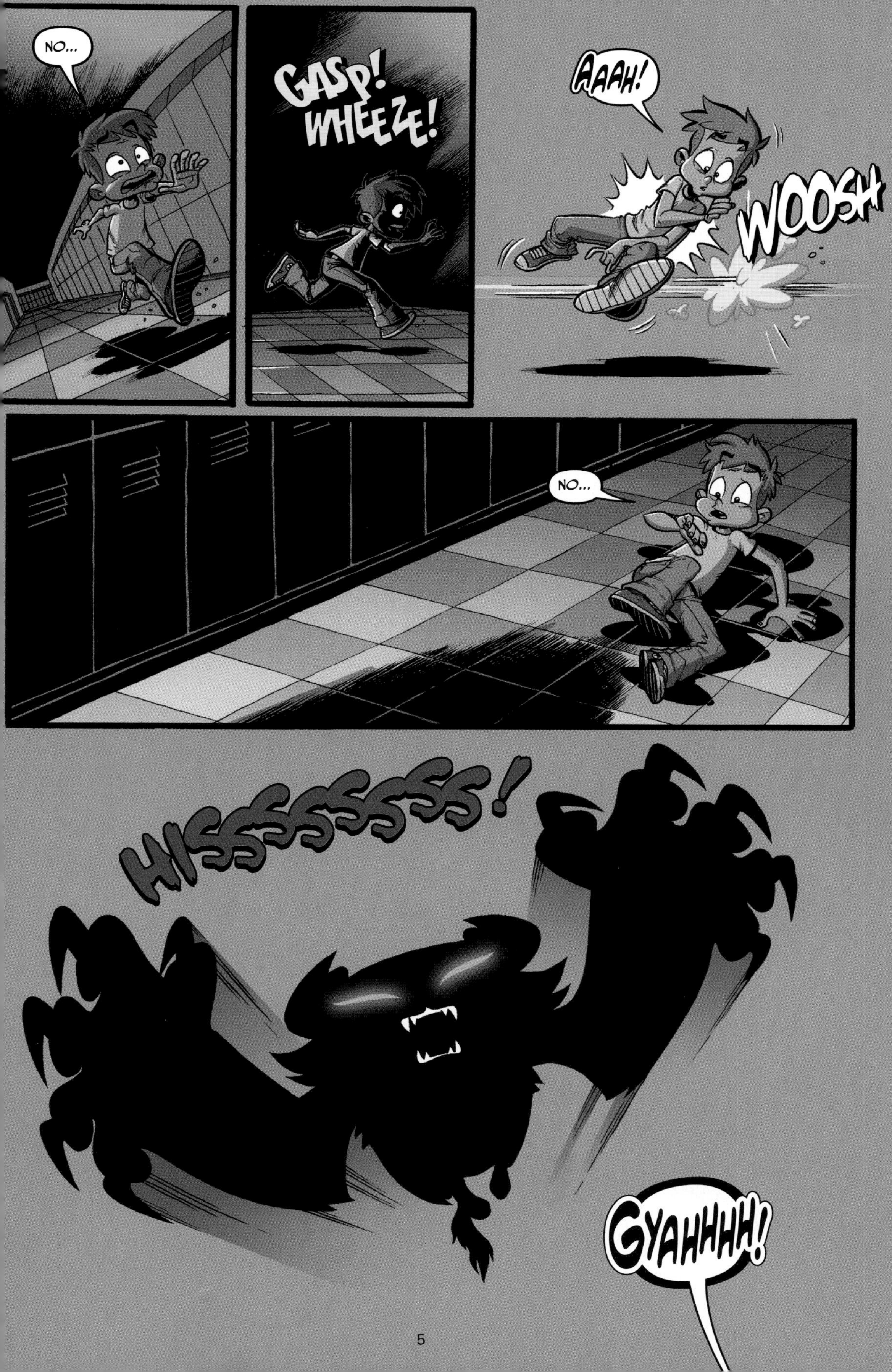
NO...
GASP! WHEEZE!
AAAH!
WOOSH
NO...
HISSSSSSSS!
GYAHHHH!

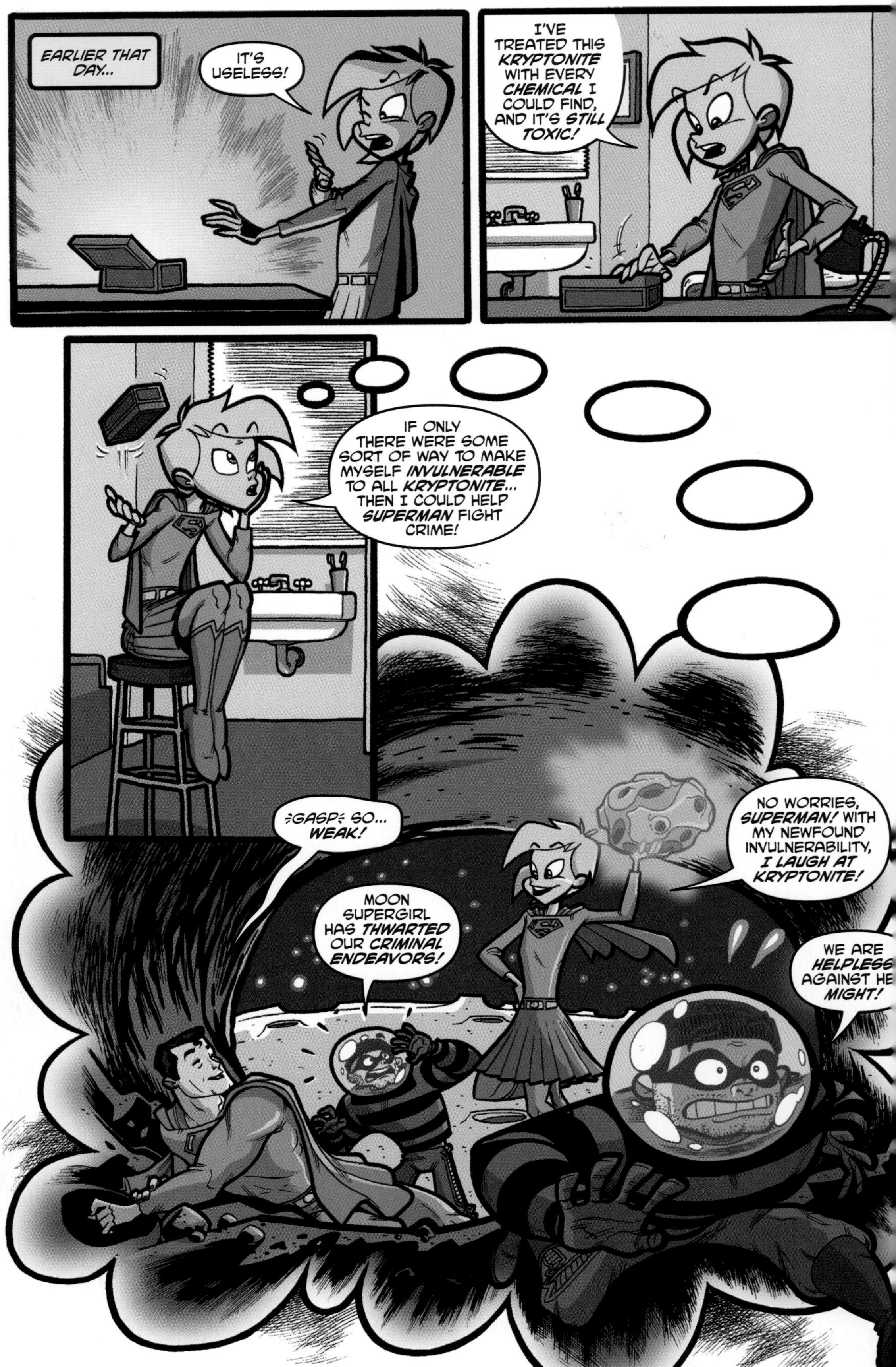
EARLIER THAT DAY...
IT'S USELESS!
I'VE TREATED THIS KRYPTONITE WITH EVERY CHEMICAL I COULD FIND, AND IT'S STILL TOXIC!
IF ONLY THERE WERE SOME SORT OF WAY TO MAKE MYSELF INVULNERABLE TO ALL KRYPTONITE... THEN I COULD HELP SUPERMAN FIGHT CRIME!
GASP SO... WEAK!
NO WORRIES, SUPERMAN! WITH MY NEWFOUND INVULNERABILITY, I LAUGH AT KRYPTONITE!
MOON SUPERGIRL HAS THWARTED OUR CRIMINAL ENDEAVORS!
WE ARE HELPLESS AGAINST HE MIGHT!

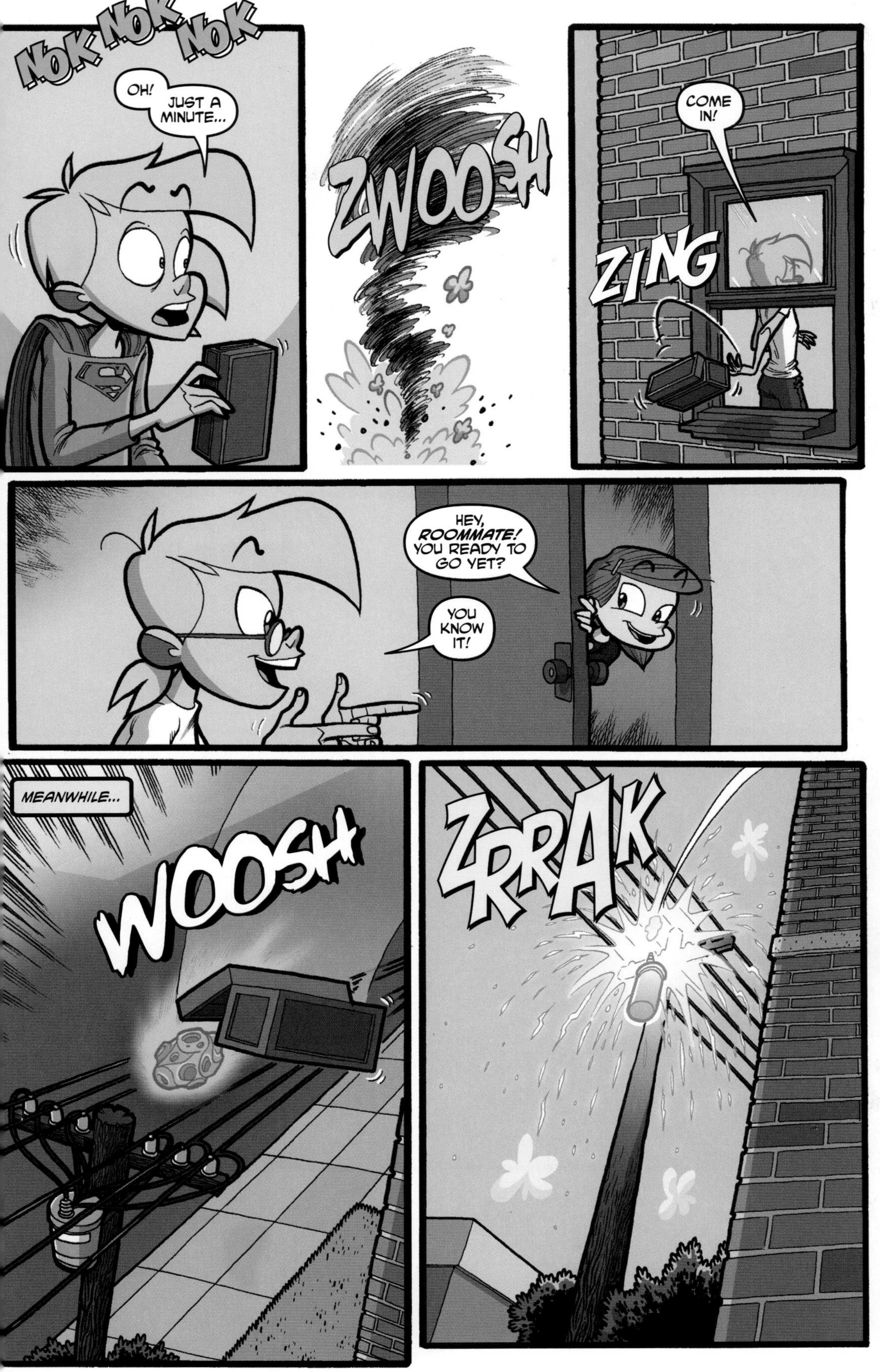
NOK NOK NOK
OH!
JUST A MINUTE...
ZWOOSH
COME IN!
ZING
HEY, ROOMMATE! YOU READY TO GO YET?
YOU KNOW IT!
MEANWHILE...
WOOSH
ZRRAK

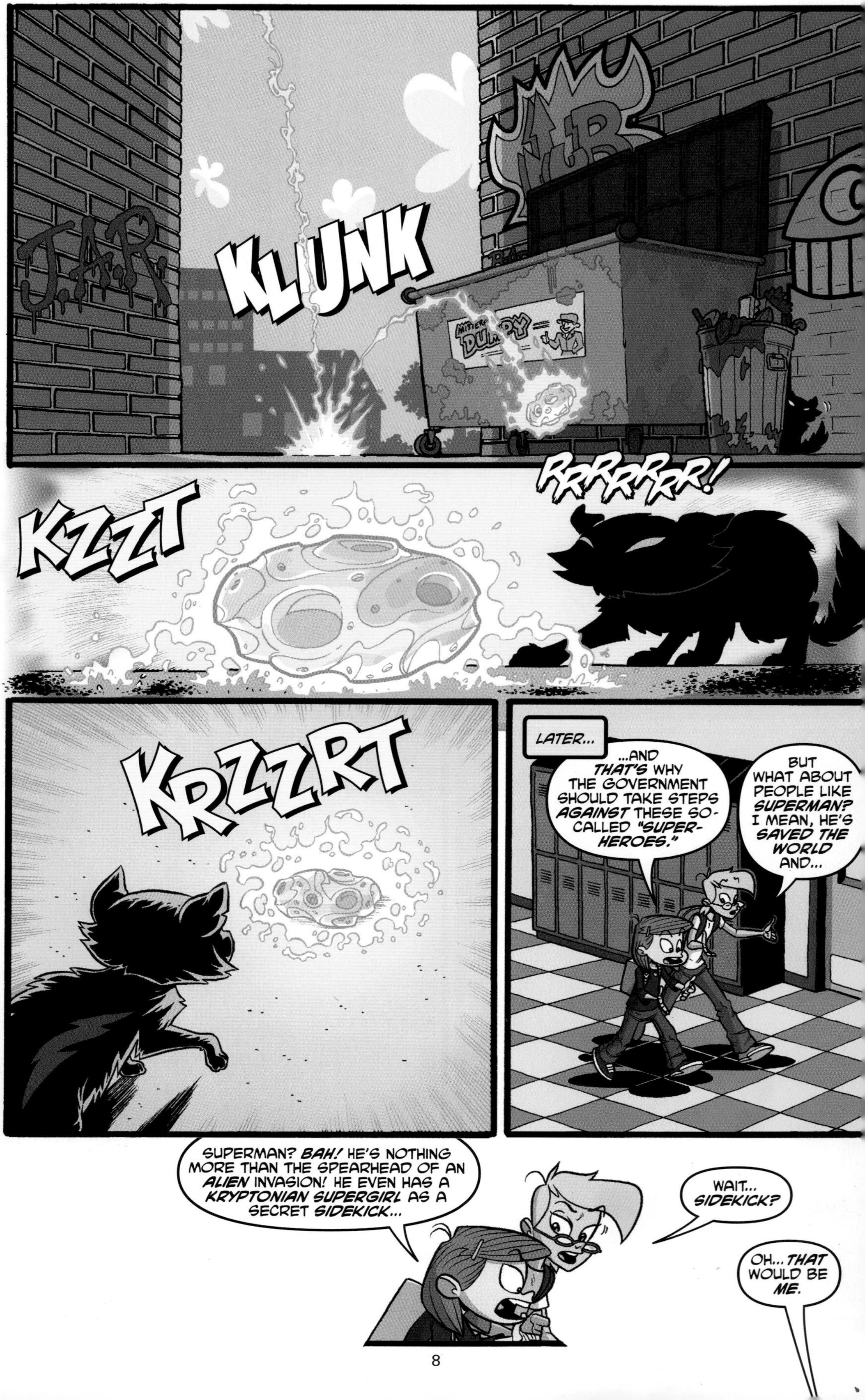
KLUNK
KZZZT
RRRRRRR!
KRZZZRT
LATER...
...AND THAT'S WHY THE GOVERNMENT SHOULD TAKE STEPS AGAINST THESE SO-CALLED "SUPER-HEROES."
BUT WHAT ABOUT PEOPLE LIKE SUPERMAN? I MEAN, HE'S SAVED THE WORLD AND...
SUPERMAN? BAH! HE'S NOTHING MORE THAN THE SPEARHEAD OF AN ALIEN INVASION! HE EVEN HAS A KRYPTONIAN SUPERGIRL AS A SECRET SIDEKICK...
WAIT... SIDEKICK?
OH... THAT WOULD BE ME.

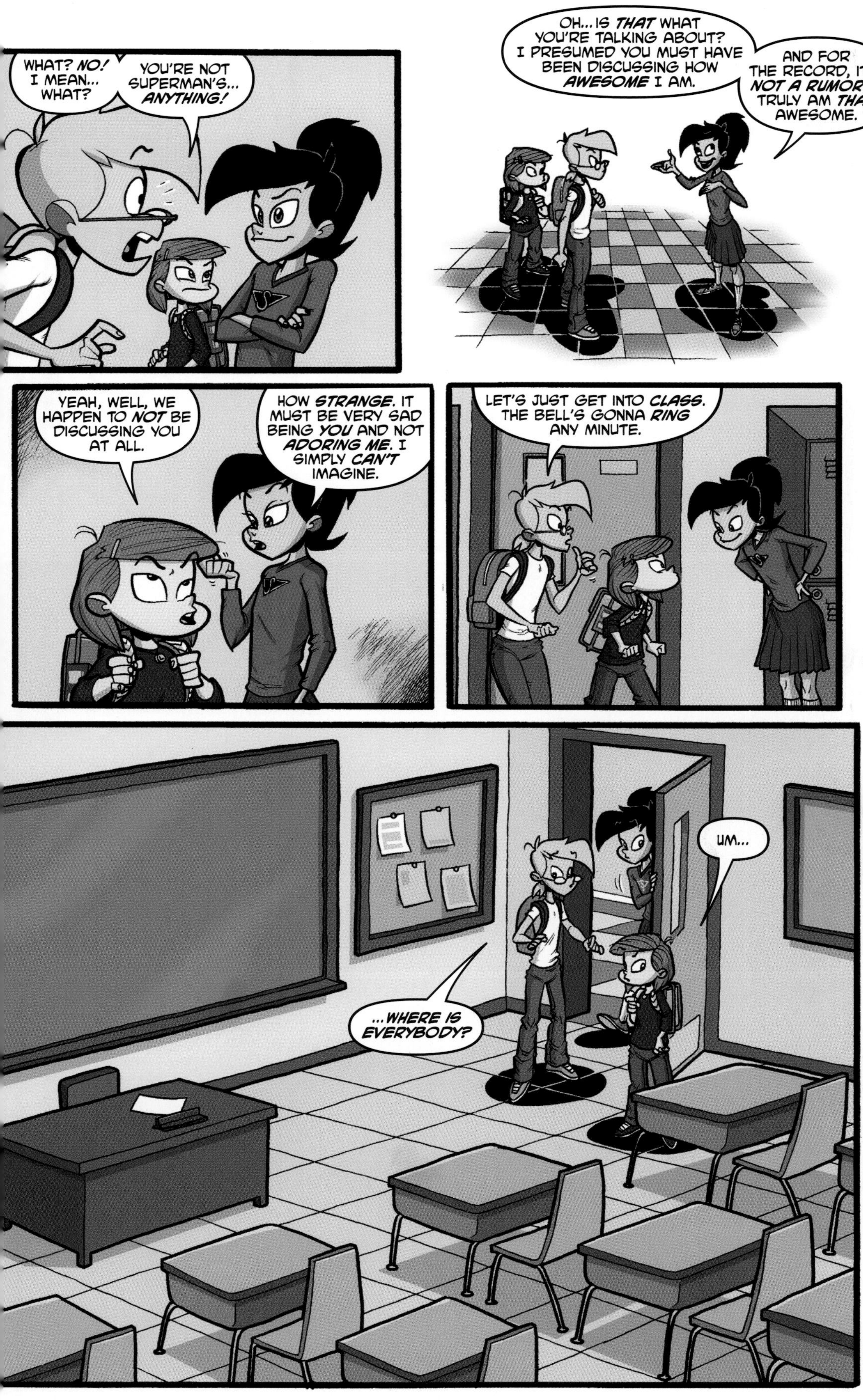
WHAT? NO! I MEAN... WHAT?
YOU'RE NOT SUPERMAN'S... ANYTHING!
OH... IS THAT WHAT YOU'RE TALKING ABOUT? I PRESUMED YOU MUST HAVE BEEN DISCUSSING HOW AWESOME I AM.
AND FOR THE RECORD, IT'S NOT A RUMOR. I TRULY AM THAT AWESOME.
YEAH, WELL, WE HAPPEN TO NOT BE DISCUSSING YOU AT ALL.
HOW STRANGE. IT MUST BE VERY SAD BEING YOU AND NOT ADORING ME. I SIMPLY CAN'T IMAGINE.
LET'S JUST GET INTO CLASS. THE BELL'S GONNA RING ANY MINUTE.
UM...
...WHERE IS EVERYBODY?

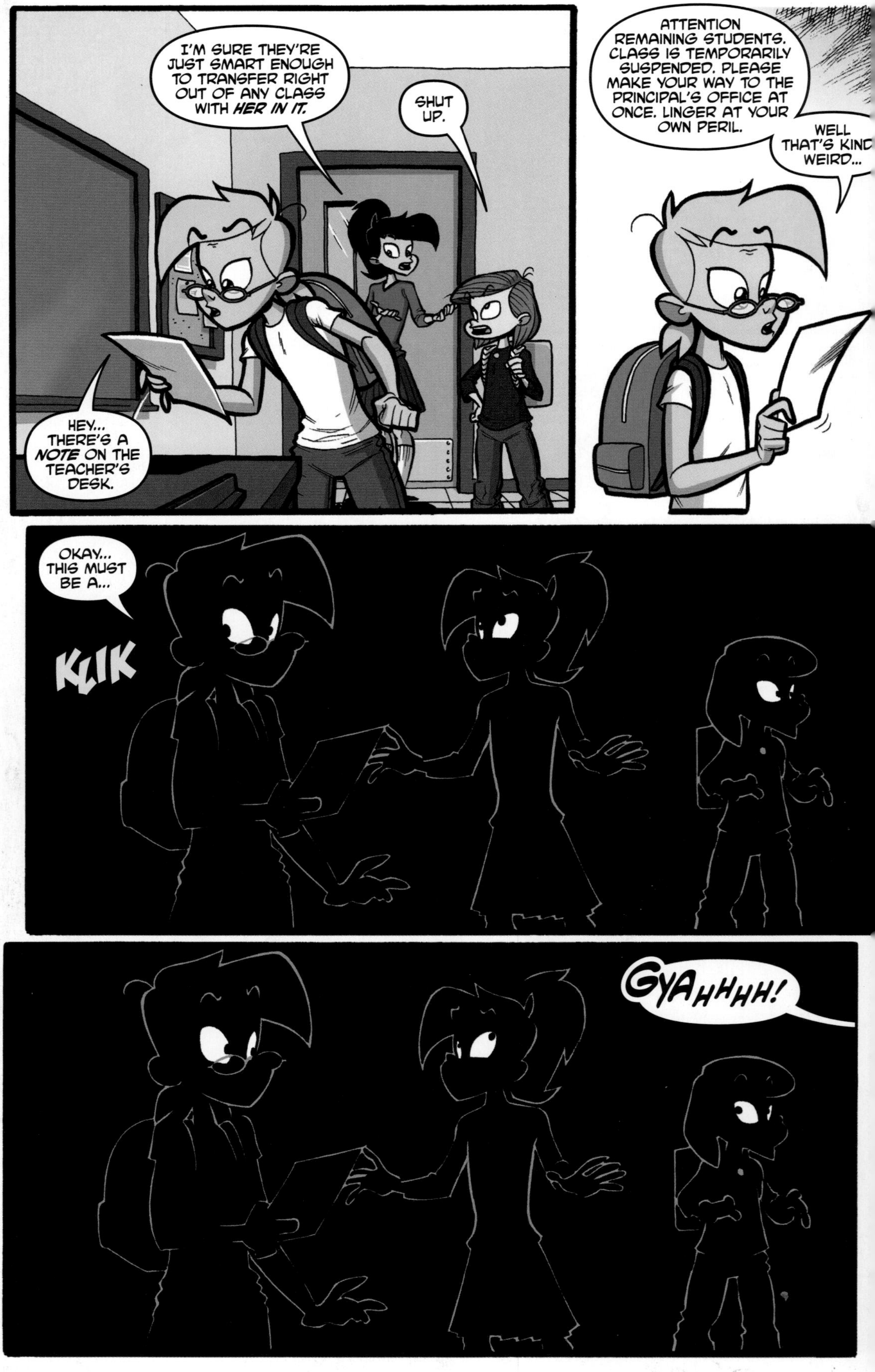
I'M SURE THEY'RE JUST SMART ENOUGH TO TRANSFER RIGHT OUT OF ANY CLASS WITH *HER IN IT.*
SHUT UP.
HEY... THERE'S A *NOTE* ON THE TEACHER'S DESK.
ATTENTION REMAINING STUDENTS. CLASS IS TEMPORARILY SUSPENDED. PLEASE MAKE YOUR WAY TO THE PRINCIPAL'S OFFICE AT ONCE. LINGER AT YOUR OWN PERIL.
WELL THAT'S KIND WEIRD...
OKAY... THIS MUST BE A...
KLIK
GYAHHHH!

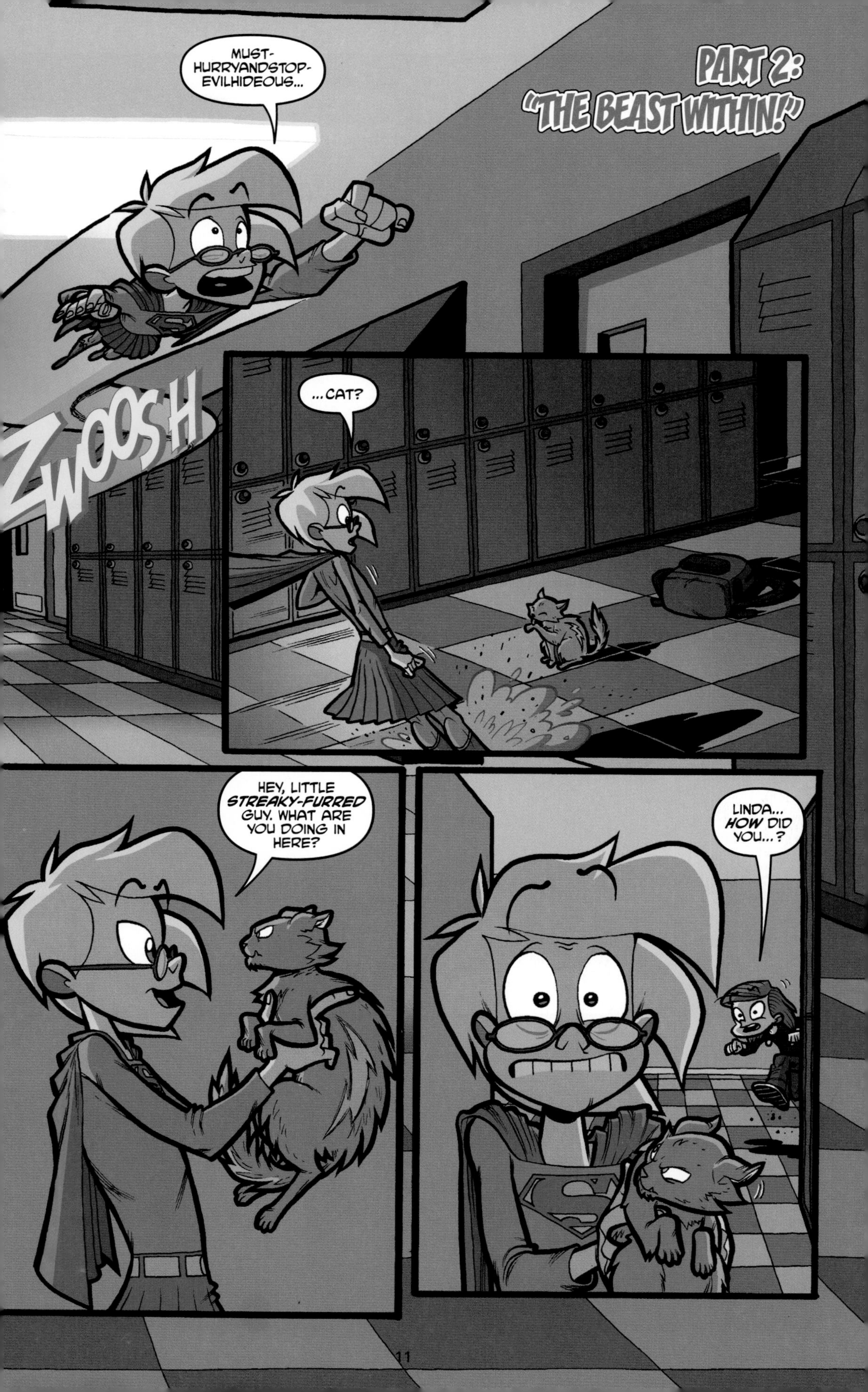
MUST-HURRYANDSTOP-EVILHIDEOUS...
PART 2: "THE BEAST WITHIN!"
ZWOOSH
...CAT?
HEY, LITTLE STREAKY-FURRED GUY. WHAT ARE YOU DOING IN HERE?
LINDA... HOW DID YOU...?

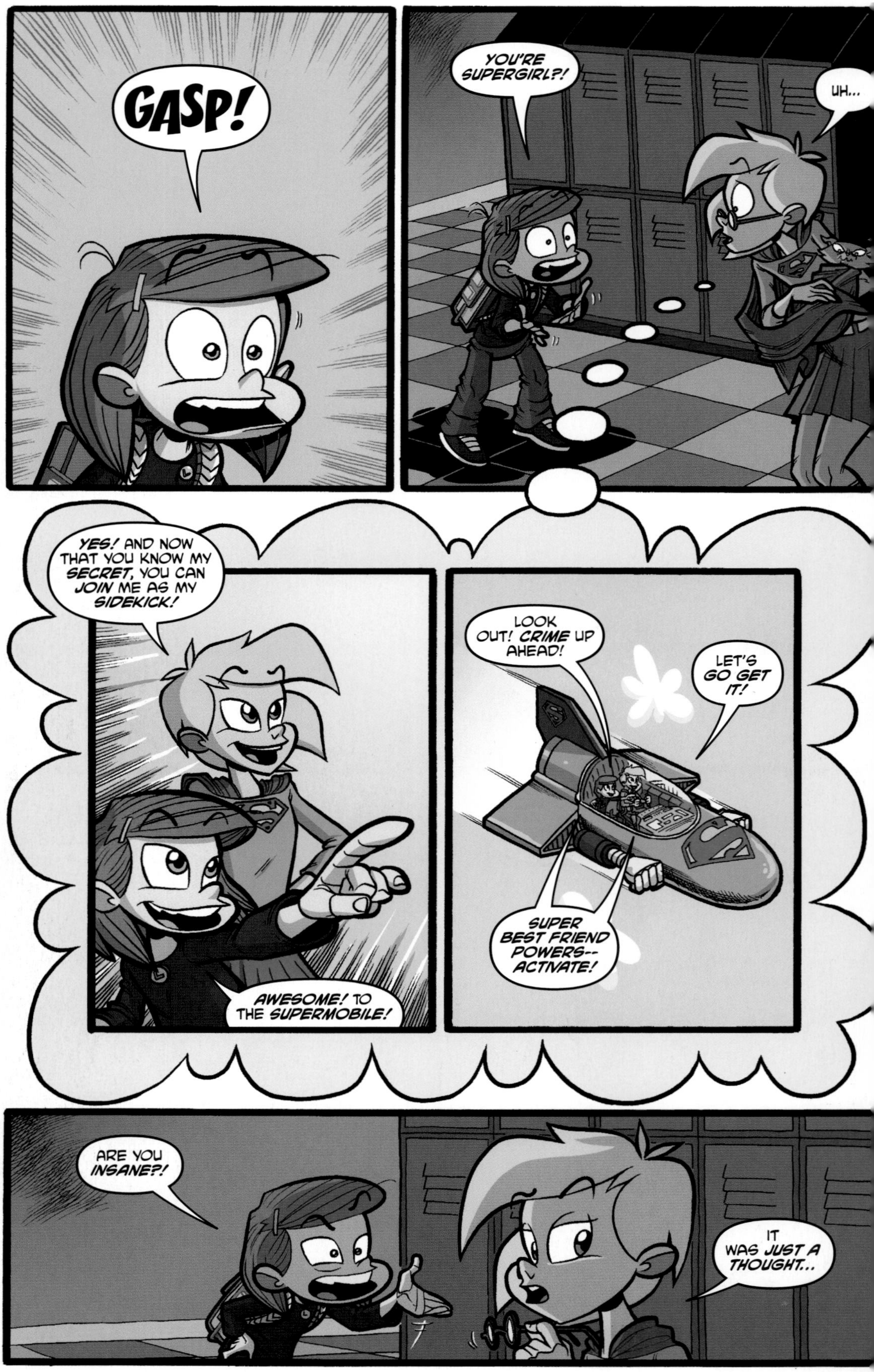
GASP!
YOU'RE SUPERGIRL?!
UH...
YES! AND NOW THAT YOU KNOW MY SECRET, YOU CAN JOIN ME AS MY SIDEKICK!
AWESOME! TO THE SUPERMOBILE!
LOOK OUT! CRIME UP AHEAD!
LET'S GO GET IT!
SUPER BEST FRIEND POWERS--ACTIVATE!
ARE YOU INSANE?!
IT WAS JUST A THOUGHT...

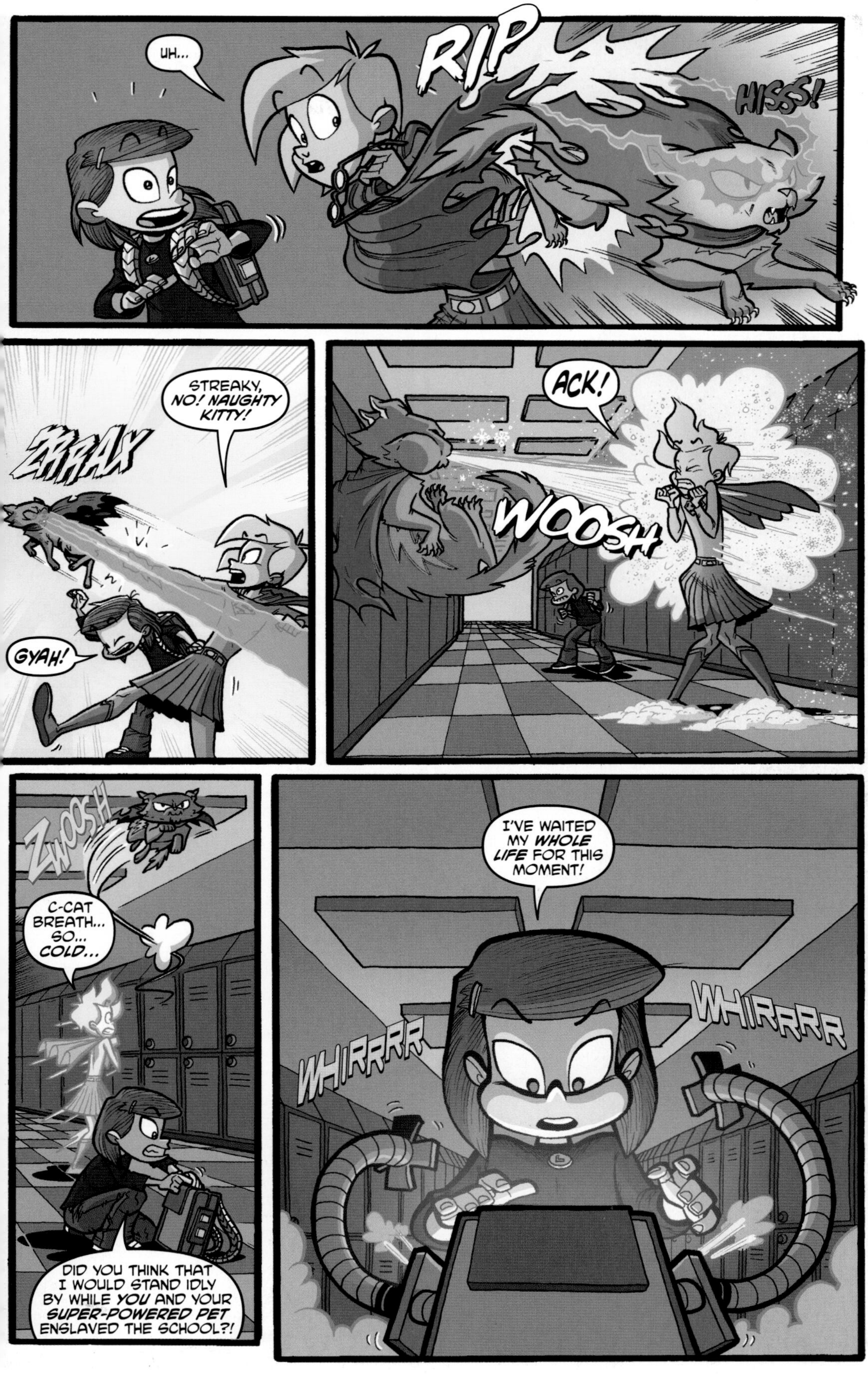
UH...
RIP
HISSS!
STREAKY, NO! NAUGHTY KITTY!
ZRRAX
GYAH!
ACK!
WOOSH
ZWOOSH
C-CAT BREATH... SO... COLD...
DID YOU THINK THAT I WOULD STAND IDLY BY WHILE YOU AND YOUR SUPER-POWERED PET ENSLAVED THE SCHOOL?!
I'VE WAITED MY WHOLE LIFE FOR THIS MOMENT!
WHIRRRR
WHIRRRR

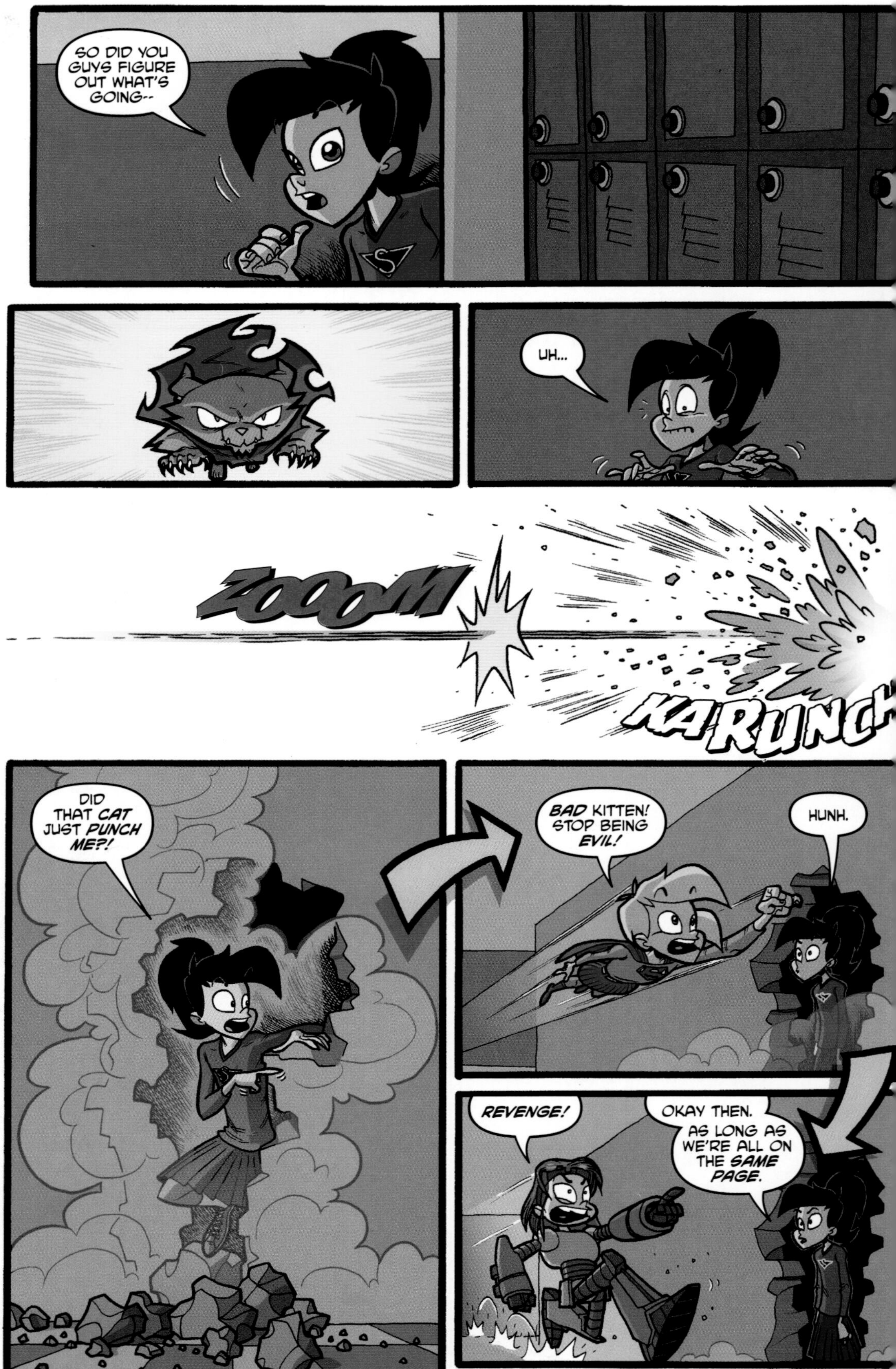
SO DID YOU GUYS FIGURE OUT WHAT'S GOING--
UH...
ZOOOOM
KA-RUNCH
DID THAT CAT JUST PUNCH ME?!
BAD KITTEN! STOP BEING EVIL!
HUNH.
REVENGE!
OKAY THEN. AS LONG AS WE'RE ALL ON THE SAME PAGE.

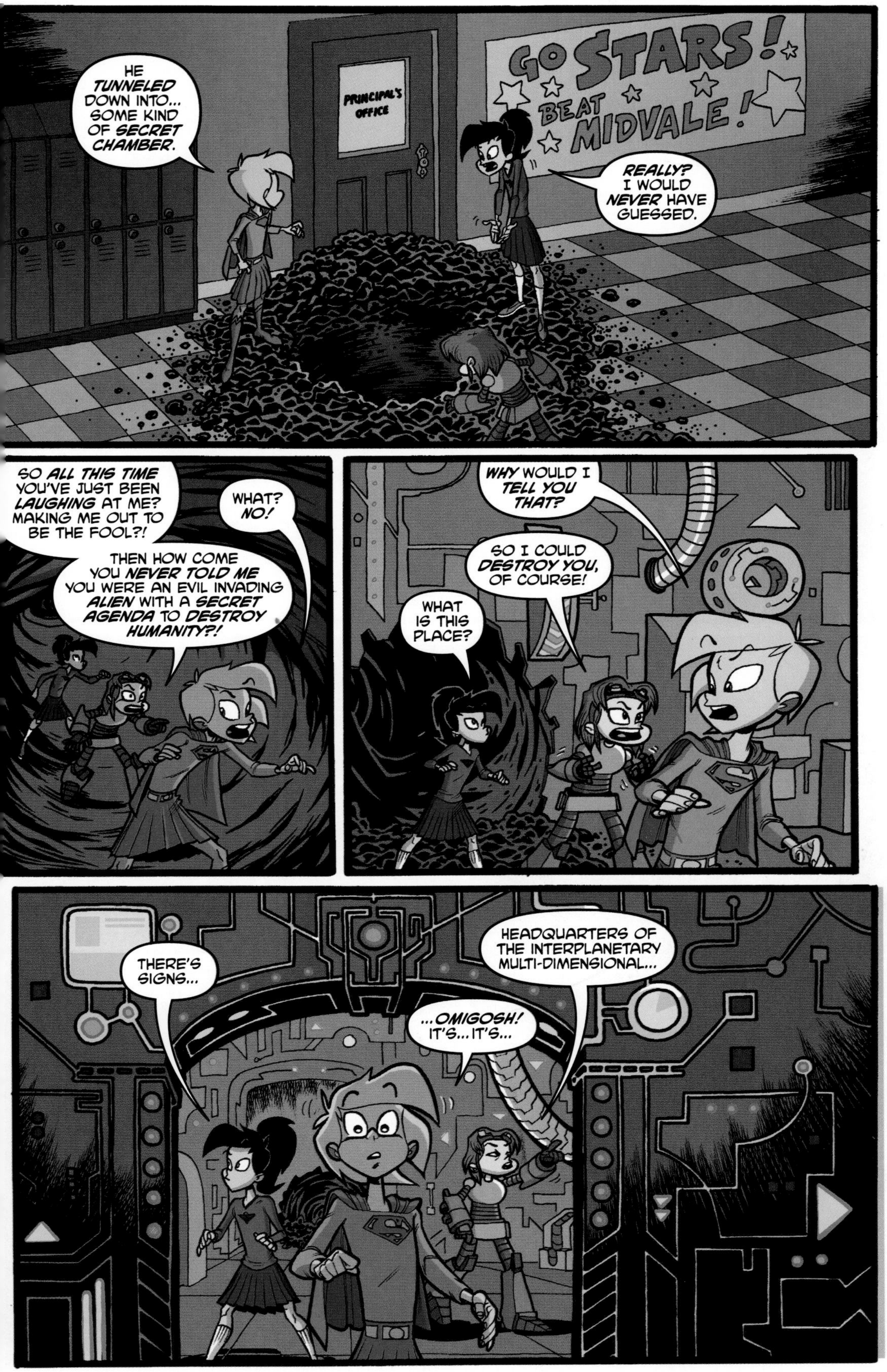

HE TUNNELED DOWN INTO... SOME KIND OF SECRET CHAMBER.
PRINCIPAL'S OFFICE
GO STARS! BEAT MIDVALE!
REALLY? I WOULD NEVER HAVE GUESSED.
SO ALL THIS TIME YOU'VE JUST BEEN LAUGHING AT ME? MAKING ME OUT TO BE THE FOOL?!
WHAT? NO!
THEN HOW COME YOU NEVER TOLD ME YOU WERE AN EVIL INVADING ALIEN WITH A SECRET AGENDA TO DESTROY HUMANITY?!
WHY WOULD I TELL YOU THAT?
SO I COULD DESTROY YOU, OF COURSE!
WHAT IS THIS PLACE?
THERE'S SIGNS...
HEADQUARTERS OF THE INTERPLANETARY MULTI-DIMENSIONAL...
...OMIGOSH! IT'S... IT'S...

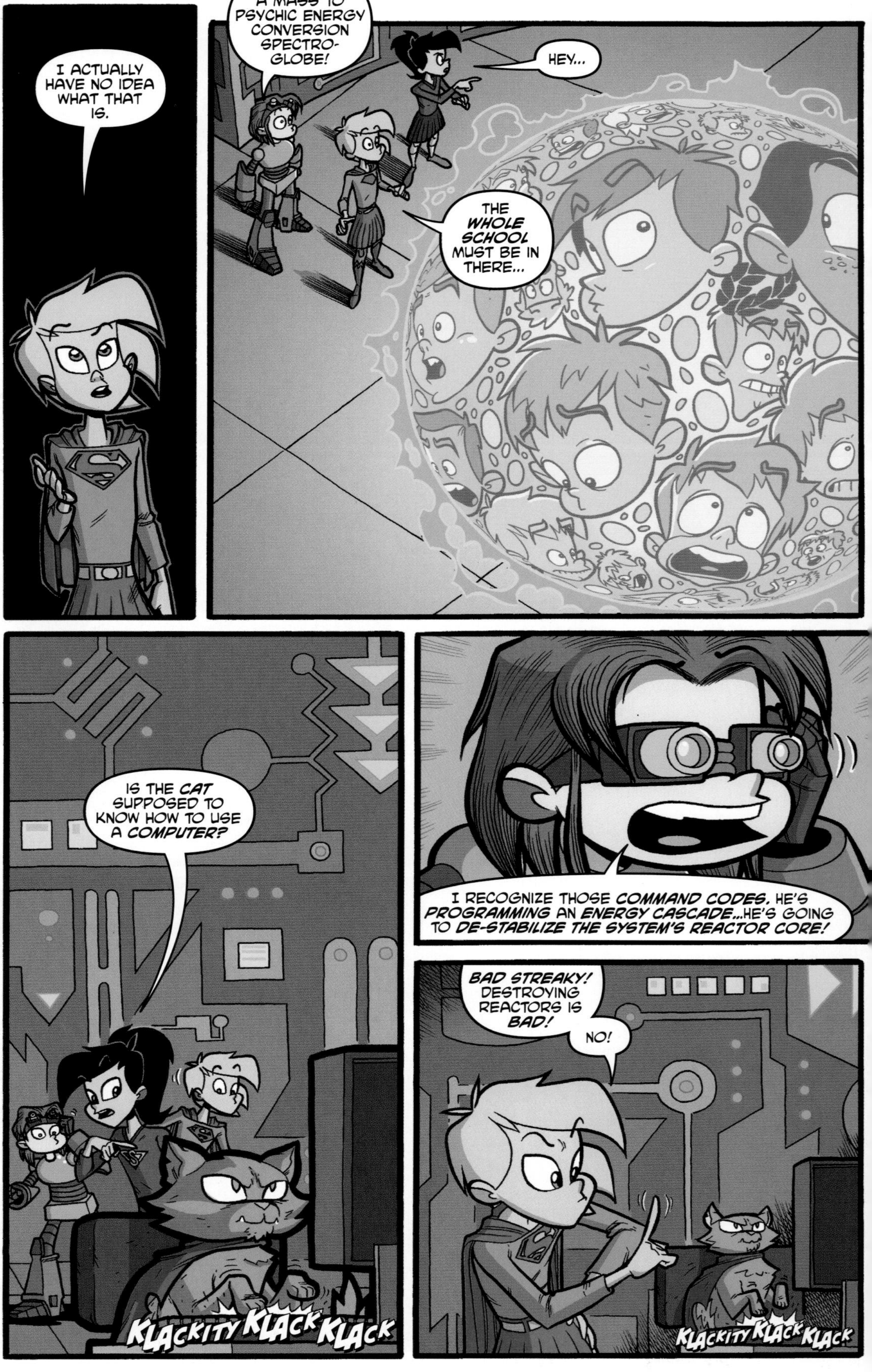
I ACTUALLY HAVE NO IDEA WHAT THAT IS.
THAT'S A MASS TO PSYCHIC ENERGY CONVERSION SPECTRO-GLOBE!
HEY...
THE *WHOLE SCHOOL* MUST BE IN THERE...
IS THE *CAT* SUPPOSED TO KNOW HOW TO USE A *COMPUTER?*
KLACKITY KLACK KLACK
I RECOGNIZE THOSE *COMMAND CODES*. HE'S *PROGRAMMING* AN *ENERGY CASCADE*...HE'S GOING TO *DE-STABILIZE THE SYSTEM'S REACTOR CORE!*
BAD STREAKY! DESTROYING REACTORS IS *BAD!*
NO!
KLACKITY KLACK KLACK

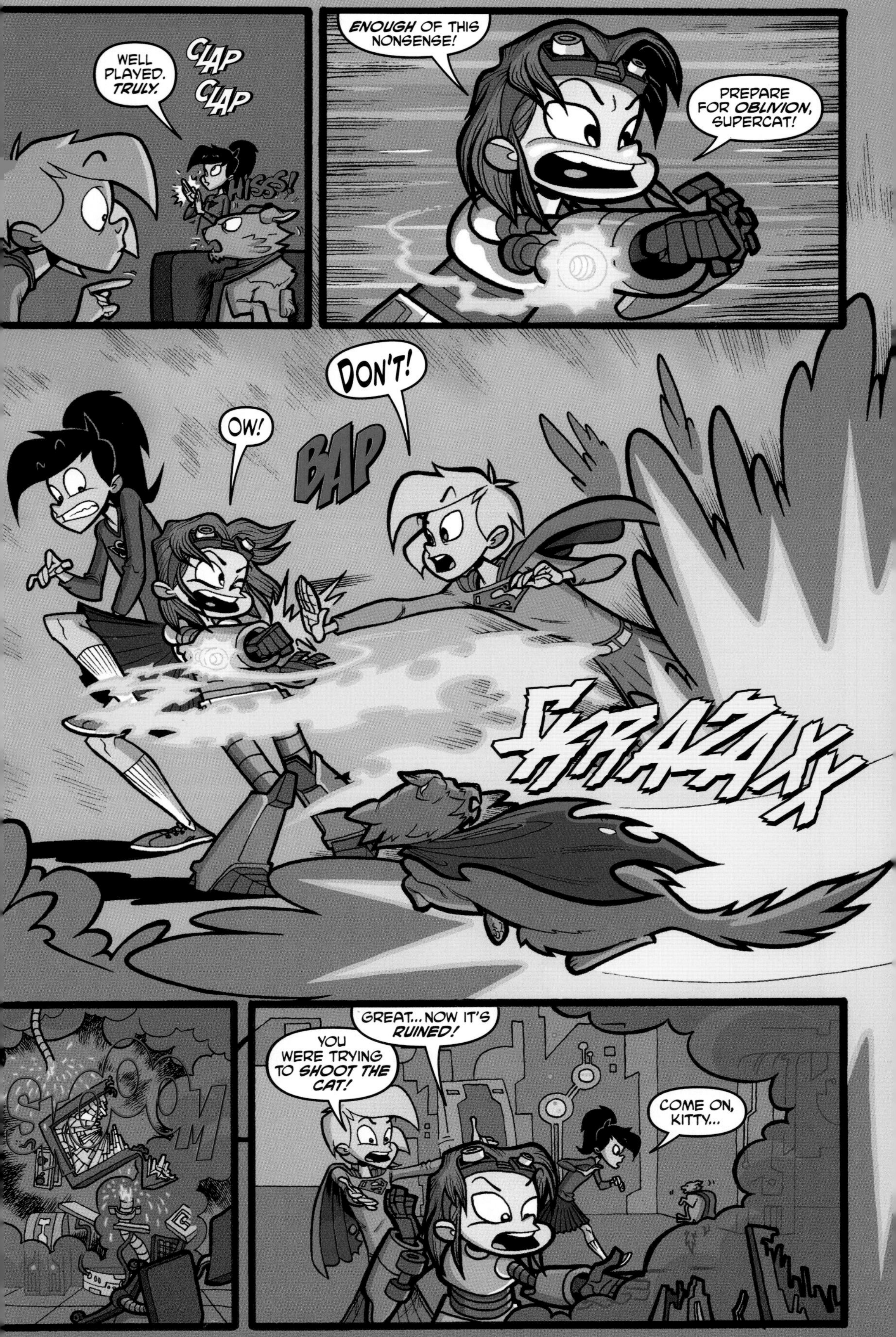
WELL PLAYED. TRULY.
CLAP CLAP
HISSS!
ENOUGH OF THIS NONSENSE!
PREPARE FOR OBLIVION, SUPERCAT!
OW!
BAP
DON'T!
SKRAZAXX
YOU WERE TRYING TO SHOOT THE CAT!
GREAT... NOW IT'S RUINED!
COME ON, KITTY...

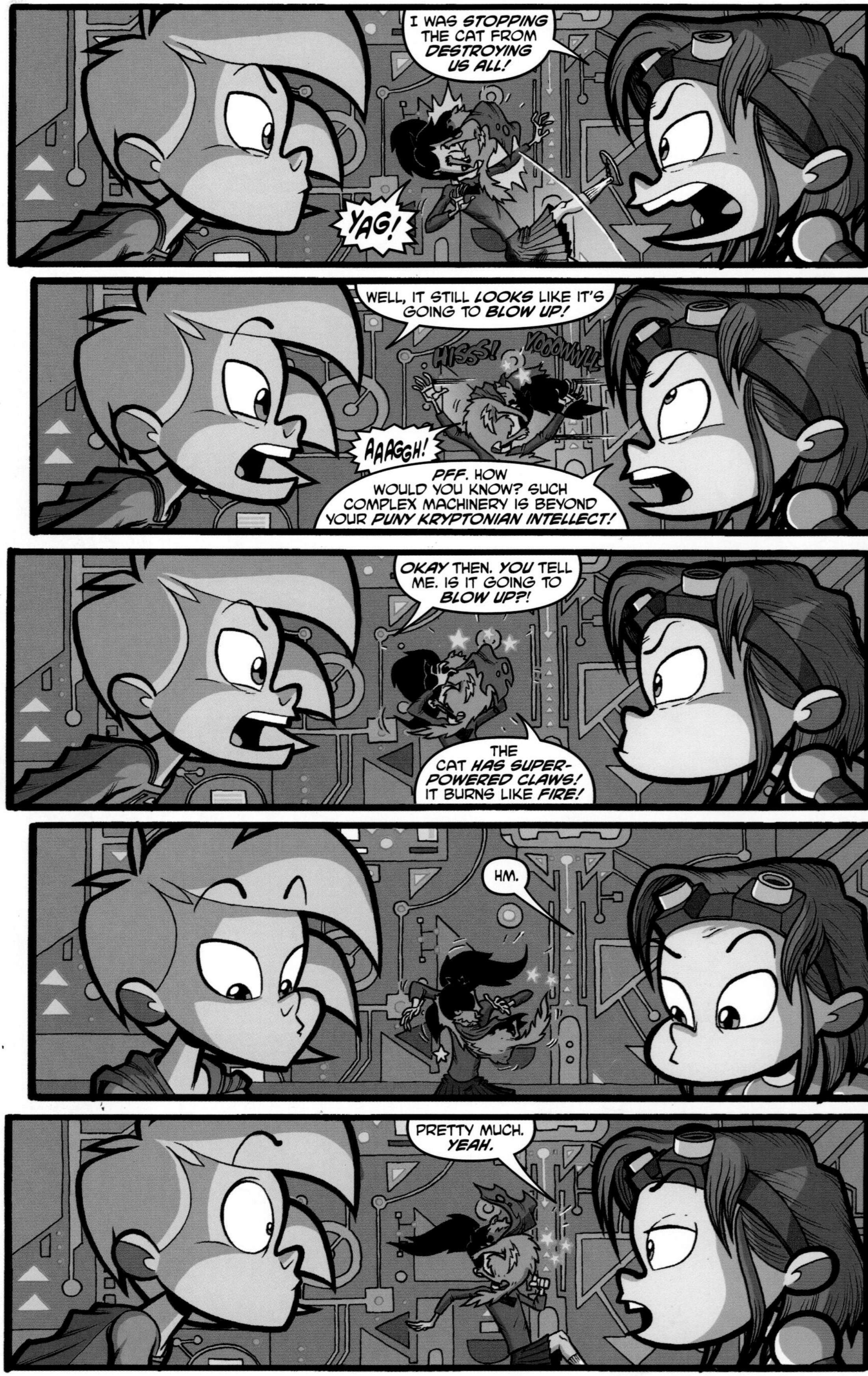
I WAS STOPPING THE CAT FROM DESTROYING US ALL!
YAG!
WELL, IT STILL LOOKS LIKE IT'S GOING TO BLOW UP!
HISSS!
YOOONWLL
AAAGGH!
PFF. HOW WOULD YOU KNOW? SUCH COMPLEX MACHINERY IS BEYOND YOUR PUNY KRYPTONIAN INTELLECT!
OKAY THEN. YOU TELL ME. IS IT GOING TO BLOW UP?!
THE CAT HAS SUPER-POWERED CLAWS! IT BURNS LIKE FIRE!
HM.
PRETTY MUCH. YEAH.

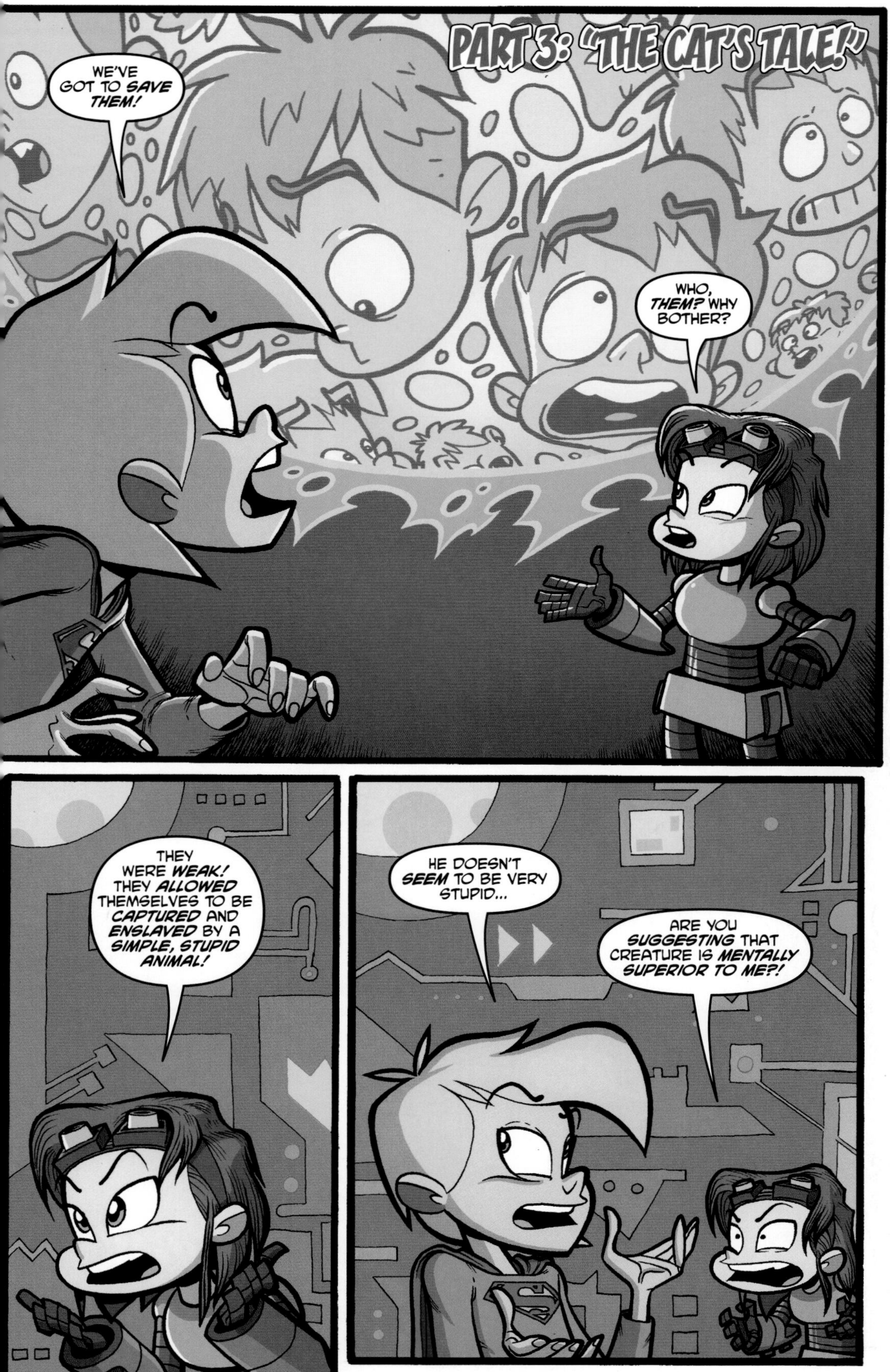
PART 3: "THE CAT'S TALE!"
WE'VE GOT TO SAVE THEM!
WHO, THEM? WHY BOTHER?
THEY WERE WEAK! THEY ALLOWED THEMSELVES TO BE CAPTURED AND ENSLAVED BY A SIMPLE, STUPID ANIMAL!
HE DOESN'T SEEM TO BE VERY STUPID...
ARE YOU SUGGESTING THAT CREATURE IS MENTALLY SUPERIOR TO ME?!

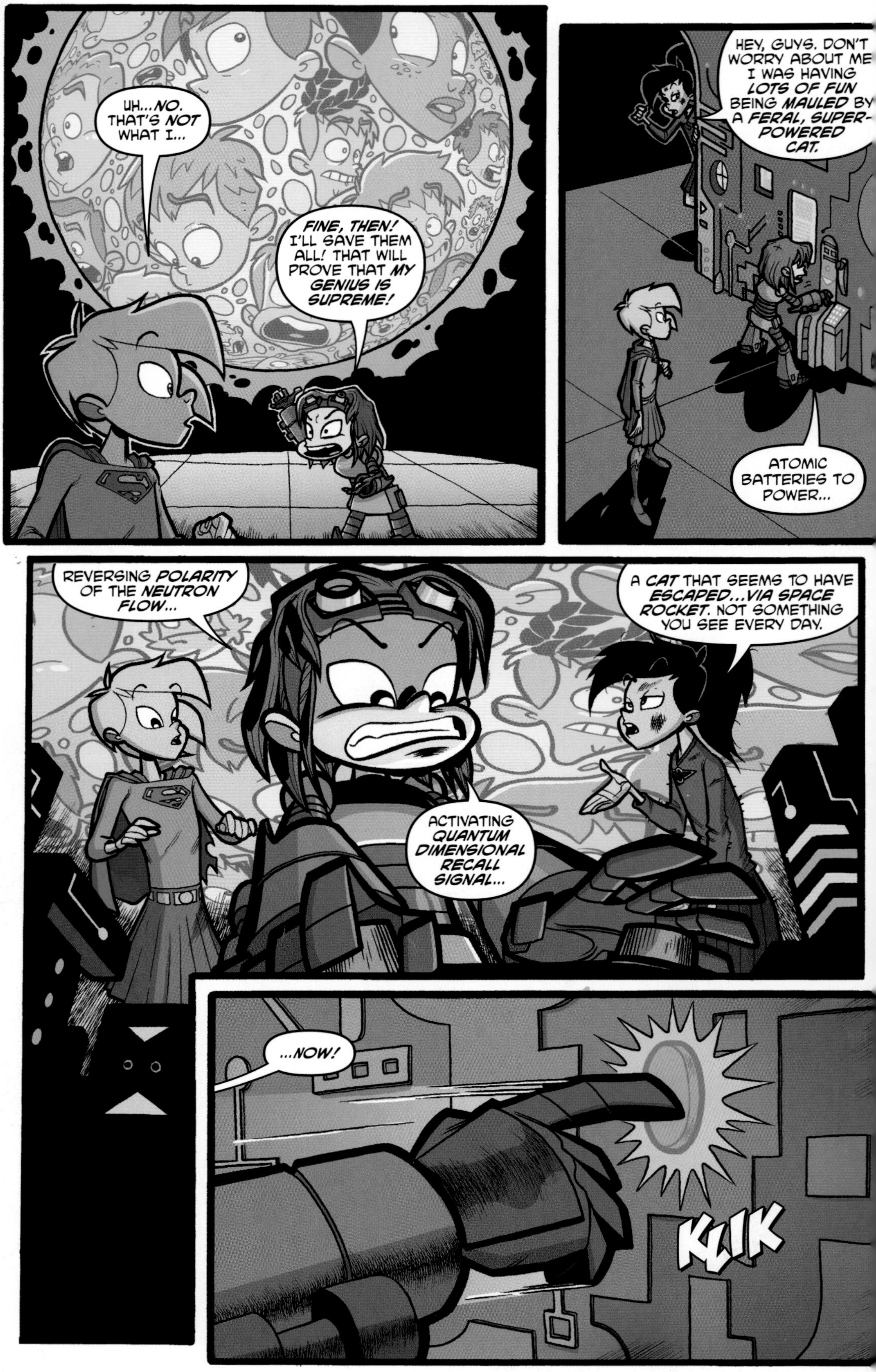
UH...NO. THAT'S NOT WHAT I...
FINE, THEN! I'LL SAVE THEM ALL! THAT WILL PROVE THAT MY GENIUS IS SUPREME!
HEY, GUYS. DON'T WORRY ABOUT ME. I WAS HAVING LOTS OF FUN BEING MAULED BY A FERAL, SUPER-POWERED CAT.
ATOMIC BATTERIES TO POWER...
REVERSING POLARITY OF THE NEUTRON FLOW...
A CAT THAT SEEMS TO HAVE ESCAPED...VIA SPACE ROCKET. NOT SOMETHING YOU SEE EVERY DAY.
ACTIVATING QUANTUM DIMENSIONAL RECALL SIGNAL...
...NOW!
KLIK

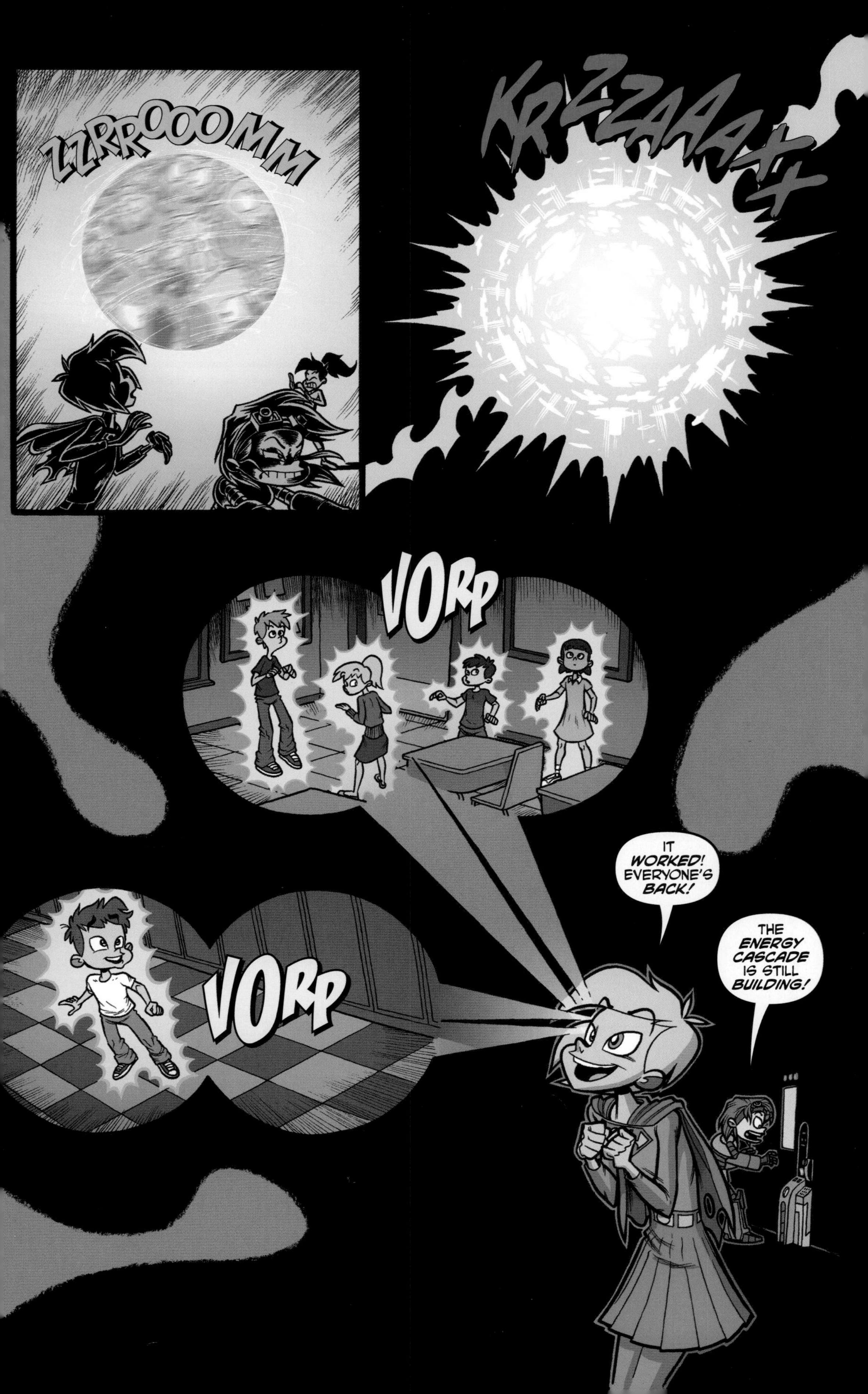
ZZRROOOMM
KRZZAAAKK
VORP
VORP
IT WORKED! EVERYONE'S BACK!
THE ENERGY CASCADE IS STILL BUILDING!

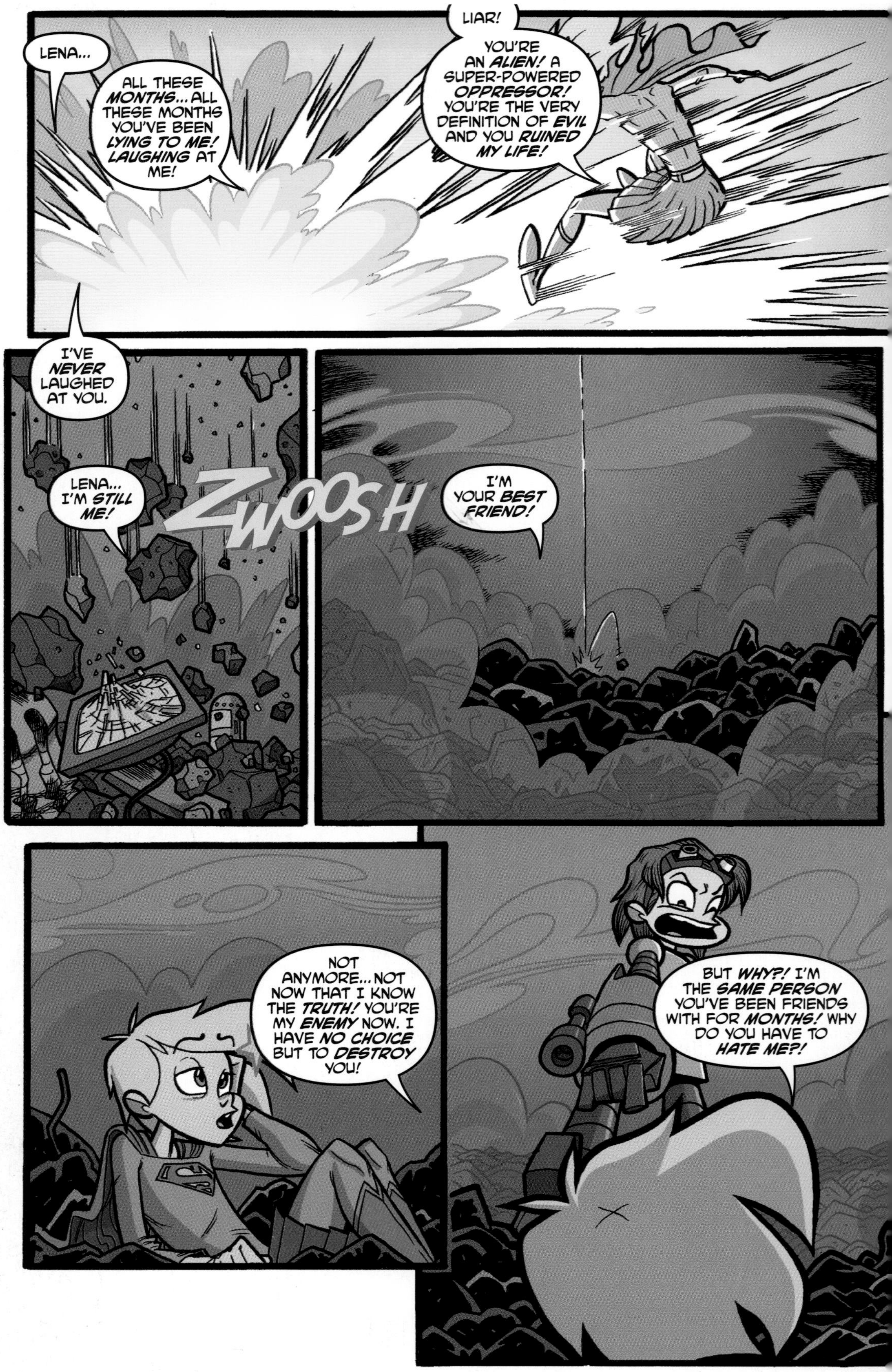
LENA...
ALL THESE MONTHS... ALL THESE MONTHS YOU'VE BEEN LYING TO ME! LAUGHING AT ME!
LIAR!
YOU'RE AN ALIEN! A SUPER-POWERED OPPRESSOR! YOU'RE THE VERY DEFINITION OF EVIL AND YOU RUINED MY LIFE!
I'VE NEVER LAUGHED AT YOU.
LENA... I'M STILL ME!
ZWOOSH
I'M YOUR BEST FRIEND!
NOT ANYMORE... NOT NOW THAT I KNOW THE TRUTH! YOU'RE MY ENEMY NOW. I HAVE NO CHOICE BUT TO DESTROY YOU!
BUT WHY?! I'M THE SAME PERSON YOU'VE BEEN FRIENDS WITH FOR MONTHS! WHY DO YOU HAVE TO HATE ME?!

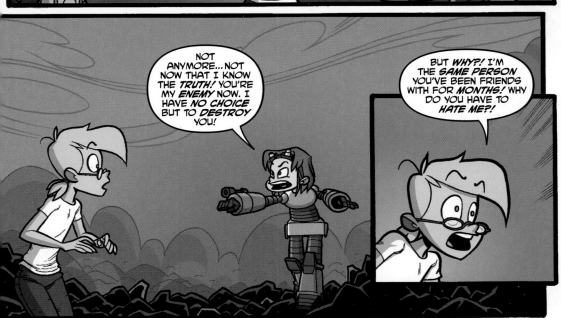

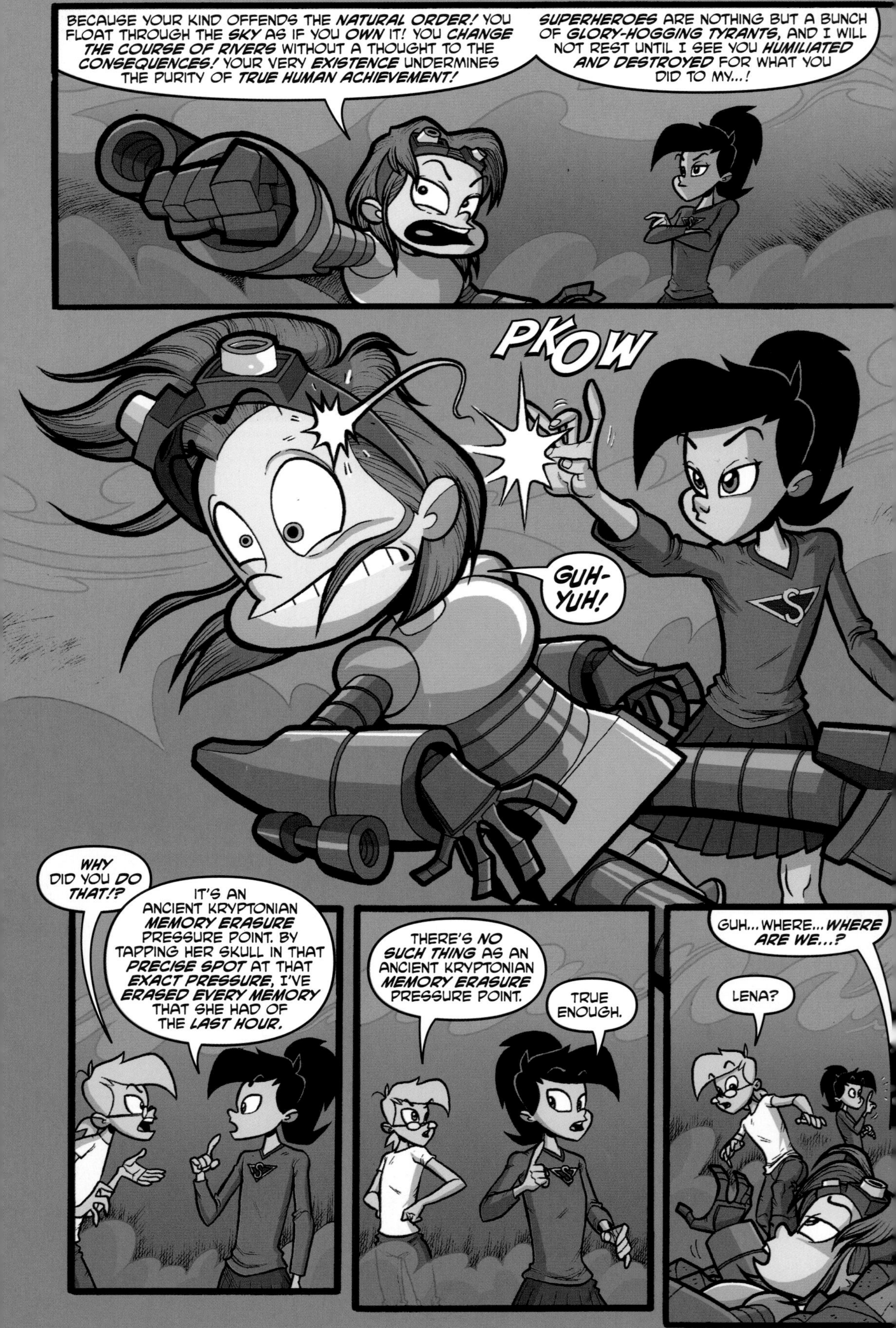
BECAUSE YOUR KIND OFFENDS THE NATURAL ORDER! YOU FLOAT THROUGH THE SKY AS IF YOU OWN IT! YOU CHANGE THE COURSE OF RIVERS WITHOUT A THOUGHT TO THE CONSEQUENCES! YOUR VERY EXISTENCE UNDERMINES THE PURITY OF TRUE HUMAN ACHIEVEMENT!
SUPERHEROES ARE NOTHING BUT A BUNCH OF GLORY-HOGGING TYRANTS, AND I WILL NOT REST UNTIL I SEE YOU HUMILIATED AND DESTROYED FOR WHAT YOU DID TO MY...!
PKOW
GUH-YUH!
WHY DID YOU DO THAT!?
IT'S AN ANCIENT KRYPTONIAN MEMORY ERASURE PRESSURE POINT. BY TAPPING HER SKULL IN THAT PRECISE SPOT AT THAT EXACT PRESSURE, I'VE ERASED EVERY MEMORY THAT SHE HAD OF THE LAST HOUR.
THERE'S NO SUCH THING AS AN ANCIENT KRYPTONIAN MEMORY ERASURE PRESSURE POINT.
TRUE ENOUGH.
GUH... WHERE... WHERE ARE WE...?
LENA?

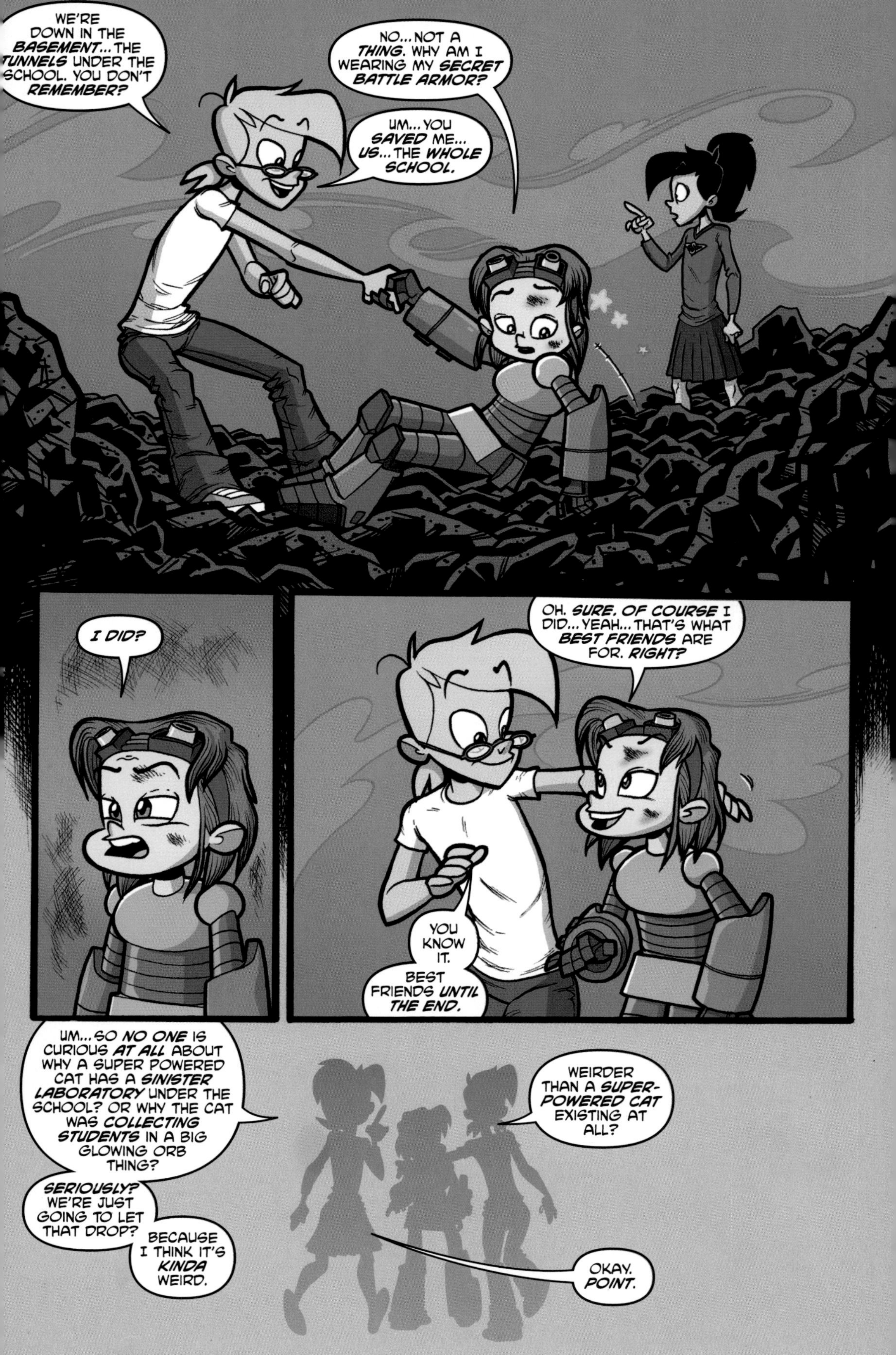
WE'RE DOWN IN THE BASEMENT... THE TUNNELS UNDER THE SCHOOL. YOU DON'T REMEMBER?
NO... NOT A THING. WHY AM I WEARING MY SECRET BATTLE ARMOR?
UM... YOU SAVED ME... US... THE WHOLE SCHOOL.
I DID?
OH. SURE. OF COURSE I DID... YEAH... THAT'S WHAT BEST FRIENDS ARE FOR. RIGHT?
YOU KNOW IT.
BEST FRIENDS UNTIL THE END.
UM... SO NO ONE IS CURIOUS AT ALL ABOUT WHY A SUPER POWERED CAT HAS A SINISTER LABORATORY UNDER THE SCHOOL? OR WHY THE CAT WAS COLLECTING STUDENTS IN A BIG GLOWING ORB THING?
SERIOUSLY? WE'RE JUST GOING TO LET THAT DROP?
BECAUSE I THINK IT'S KINDA WEIRD.
WEIRDER THAN A SUPER-POWERED CAT EXISTING AT ALL?
OKAY. POINT.

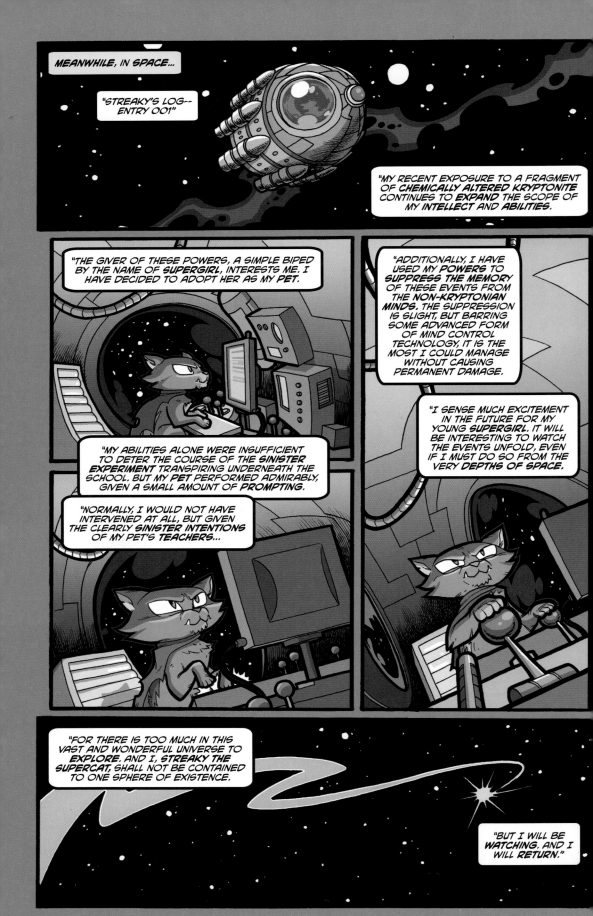

MEANWHILE, IN SPACE...

"STREAKY'S LOG--
ENTRY 001"

"MY RECENT EXPOSURE TO A FRAGMENT OF *CHEMICALLY ALTERED KRYPTONITE* CONTINUES TO *EXPAND* THE SCOPE OF MY *INTELLECT* AND *ABILITIES.*

"THE GIVER OF THESE POWERS, A SIMPLE BIPED BY THE NAME OF *SUPERGIRL,* INTERESTS ME. I HAVE DECIDED TO ADOPT HER AS MY *PET.*

"MY ABILITIES ALONE WERE INSUFFICIENT TO DETER THE COURSE OF THE *SINISTER EXPERIMENT* TRANSPIRING UNDERNEATH THE SCHOOL. BUT MY *PET* PERFORMED ADMIRABLY, GIVEN A SMALL AMOUNT OF *PROMPTING.*

"NORMALLY, I WOULD NOT HAVE INTERVENED AT ALL, BUT GIVEN THE CLEARLY *SINISTER INTENTIONS* OF MY PET'S *TEACHERS...*

"ADDITIONALLY, I HAVE USED MY *POWERS* TO *SUPPRESS THE MEMORY* OF THESE EVENTS FROM THE *NON-KRYPTONIAN MINDS.* THE SUPPRESSION IS SLIGHT, BUT BARRING SOME ADVANCED FORM OF MIND CONTROL TECHNOLOGY, IT IS THE MOST I COULD MANAGE WITHOUT CAUSING PERMANENT DAMAGE.

"I SENSE MUCH EXCITEMENT IN THE FUTURE FOR MY YOUNG *SUPERGIRL.* IT WILL BE INTERESTING TO WATCH THE EVENTS UNFOLD, EVEN IF I MUST DO SO FROM THE VERY *DEPTHS* OF SPACE.

"FOR THERE IS TOO MUCH IN THIS VAST AND WONDERFUL UNIVERSE TO *EXPLORE.* AND I, STREAKY THE *SUPERCAT,* SHALL NOT BE CONTAINED TO ONE SPHERE OF EXISTENCE.

"BUT I WILL BE *WATCHING. AND I WILL RETURN."*

CREATORS

LANDRY Q. WALKER WRITER

Landry Q. Walker is a comics writer whose projects include *Supergirl: Cosmic Adventures in the 8th Grade* and more. He has also written *Batman: The Brave and the Bold*, the comic book adventures of The Incredibles, and contributed stories to *Disney Adventures* magazine and the gaming website Elder-Geek.

ERIC JONES ARTIST

Eric Jones is a professional comic book artist whose work for DC Comics includes *Batman: The Brave and the Bold, Supergirl: Cosmic Adventures in the 8th Grade, Cartoon Network Action Pack*, and more.

JOEY MASON COLORIST

Joey Mason is an illustrator, animation artist, and comic book colorist. His work for DC Comics includes *Supergirl: Cosmic Adventures in the 8th Grade*, as well as set designs for *Green Lantern: The Animated Series*.

GLOSSARY

agenda [uh-JEN-duh]-a list of things that need to be done or discussed

endeavors [en-DEV-urz]-serious attempts or efforts

feral [FER-uhl]-having escaped from domestication and become wild

humanity [hyoo-MAN-uh-tee]-all human beings

invulnerable [in-VUHL-nur-uh-buhl]-impossible to wound, injure, or damage

Kryptonite [KRIP-tuh-nite]-a radioactive material from the planet Krypton, able to weaken the superpowers of Superman and Supergirl

oblivion [oh-BLIH-vee-uhn]-the state of being forgotten

peril [PER-uhl]-the state of being in danger of injury, loss, or destruction

revenge [ri-VENJ]-a desire to pay back injury for injury

thwarted [THWOR-tihd]-defeated the hopes, desires, or plans of something

toxic [TOK-sik]-poisonous

VISUAL QUESTIONS & PROMPTS

1. Comic book creators can tell a story using very few words. Describe what is happening in the panels below [from page 14]. What clues helped you follow the story from one panel to the next?

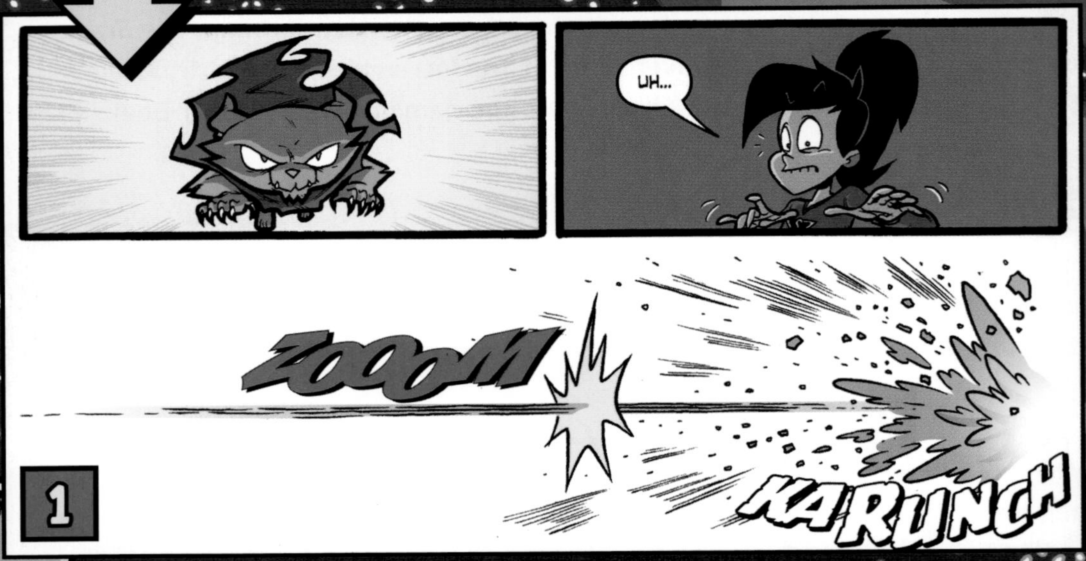
UH...
ZOOOM
KARUNCH
1

2. Study the panels at right from page 10. Why is the bottom panel colored darker than the others? Describe at least two clues that helped you reach your conclusion.

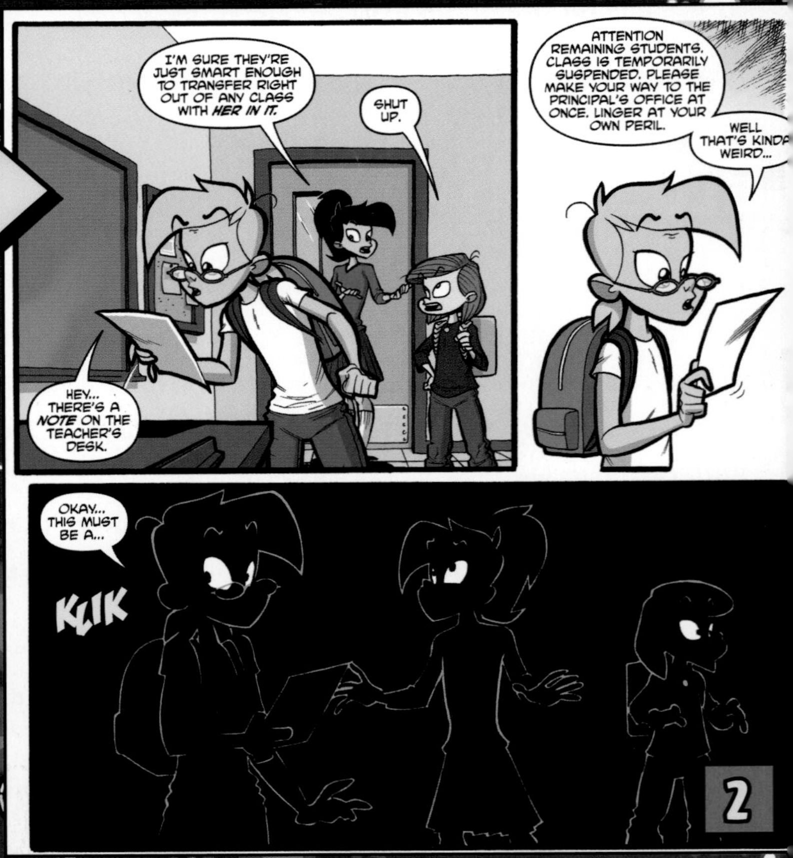
I'M SURE THEY'RE JUST SMART ENOUGH TO TRANSFER RIGHT OUT OF ANY CLASS WITH HER IN IT.
SHUT UP.
HEY... THERE'S A NOTE ON THE TEACHER'S DESK.
ATTENTION REMAINING STUDENTS. CLASS IS TEMPORARILY SUSPENDED. PLEASE MAKE YOUR WAY TO THE PRINCIPAL'S OFFICE AT ONCE. LINGER AT YOUR OWN PERIL.
WELL THAT'S KINDA WEIRD...
OKAY... THIS MUST BE A...
KLIK
2

3. The way a character's eyes and mouth are illustrated can tell a lot about the emotions he or she is feeling. How do you think Supergirl is feeling in the panel at right [from page 11]? Describe how you can tell.

LINDA... HOW DID YOU...?

3

4. In comic books, sound effects [also known as SFX] are used to show sounds, such as an explosion. Make a list of all the sound effects in this book, and then write a definition for each term. Soon, you'll have your own SFX dictionary!

SKROOOM

GUH!

4

5. Do you think Belinda needed to erase Lena's memory? Could Linda and Lena have saved their friendship in another way? If so, how?

PKOW

GUH-YUH!

5

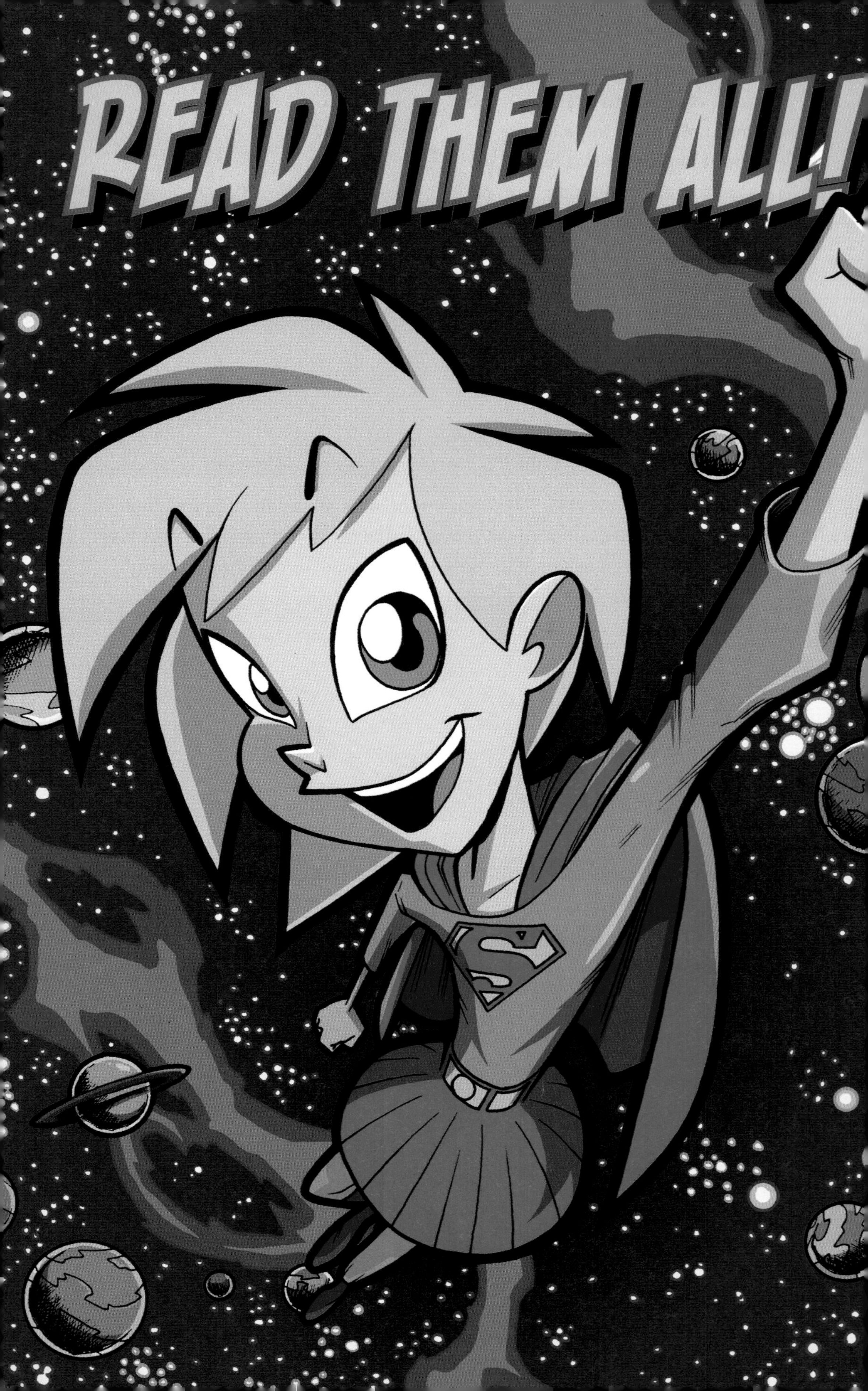
READ THEM ALL!

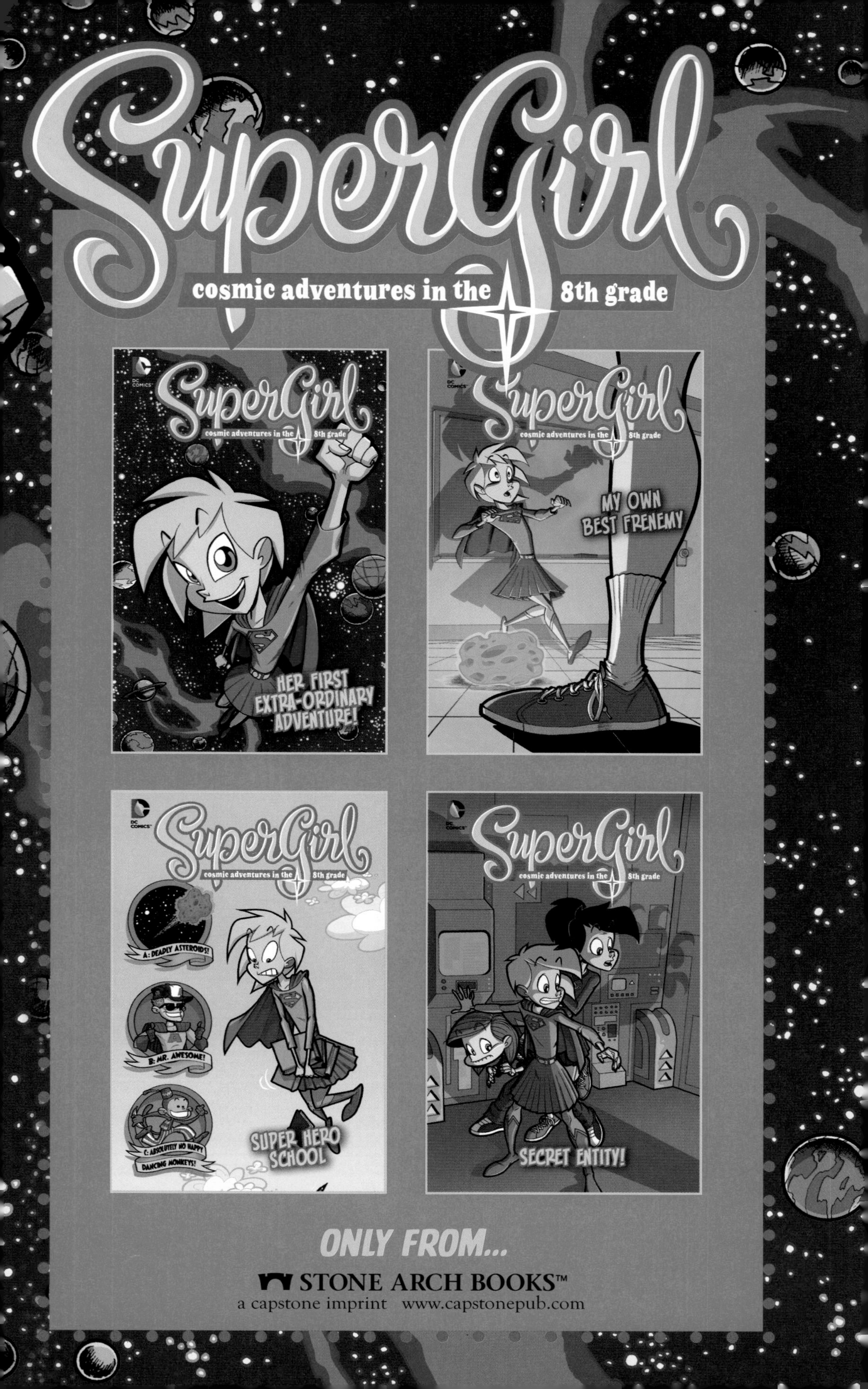
SuperGirl
cosmic adventures in the 8th grade
DC COMICS
SuperGirl
cosmic adventures in the 8th grade
HER FIRST EXTRA-ORDINARY ADVENTURE!
DC COMICS
SuperGirl
cosmic adventures in the 8th grade
MY OWN BEST FRENEMY
DC COMICS
SuperGirl
cosmic adventures in the 8th grade
A: DEADLY ASTEROIDS!
B: MR. AWESOME!
C: ABSOLUTELY NO HAPPY DANCING MONKEYS!
SUPER HERO SCHOOL
DC COMICS
SuperGirl
cosmic adventures in the 8th grade
SECRET ENTITY!
ONLY FROM...
STONE ARCH BOOKS™
a capstone imprint www.capstonepub.com

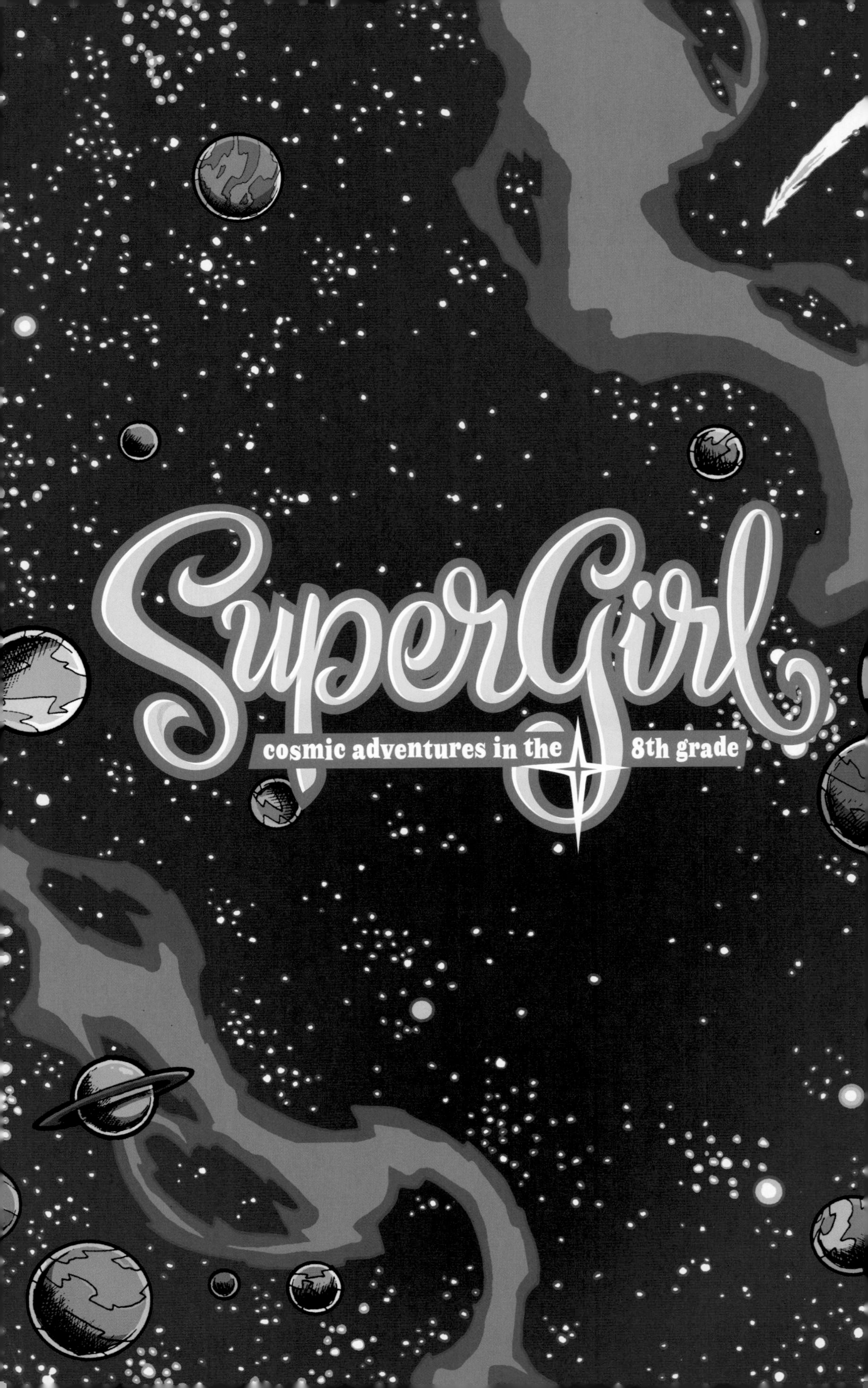
SuperGirl
cosmic adventures in the 8th grade